Rockstar's Girl

written by K.T. Fisher

To Katharine Bozier

Thankyou for loving Jax as much as I do!
Get ready for a little hotness!

K.T. Fisher

Rockstar's Girl
(Book 2 in the Decoy Series)

Copyright @2013 Kellie Fisher
Cover art @2013 CT COVER CREATIONS

Follow me on Twitter
https://www.twitter.com/KTFisher_Author

Like my Facebook page
https://www.facebook.com/#!/pages/KTFisher/490003474414733?fref=ts

Take a look at my cover designers page at
http://www.ctcovercreations.com

This is a work of fiction. Names, characters, places and incidents are either the product of the author's imagination or are used fictitiously. Any resemblance to any actual persons living or dead, businesses and events or locales are entirely coincidental.

A message from K.T.Fisher

Before I say anything I just want to say a big thank you to my family for dealing with me while I was writing this book. The many times I have been busy writing and thinking constantly about what to write next. You guys are my rock and I love you all.

I also want to thank all my readers! You guys are awesome! When I wrote *Rockstar Daddy* I didn't think it would sell as well as it did. I love writing so I just wrote it as a hobby and you all turned my dream into a reality and I thank you so much. I loved writing *Rockstar's Girl* and I hope you all love reading it.

Another big thank you to my proof readers. You know who you are. Without you my book wouldn't be as great as it is and I really thank you a lot.

Lastly I think we can all clap for Clarise Tan who designed *Rockstar Daddy's* new cover and also *Rockstar's Girl's* wonderful cover. I think I speak for everyone when I say they are beautiful.

Chapter 1

~Kendal~

The drive back home was quiet. Maisy drove me home whilst I just sat there staring out of the window. I've sent an apology text to Sophie, and she assures me everything is fine. She wants me and Jax to sort everything out and wishes me luck. When I reply back, I tell her to stop thinking about me and enjoy her honeymoon. She shouldn't be worrying about me. I feel terrible for what has just happened at her house, the day after her wedding and just before she leaves for her honeymoon.

I say my thanks to Maisy and wave goodbye to her as she gets into Jessica's car. Jessica is driving her back to Sophie's so she can get her car, I appreciate what they're doing to help me. They wanted to stay, but I just want to be alone. Luckily my mum has just text to ask if she can have Finley over for a little while longer.

When I walk in my front door, I catch a glimpse of my reflection in the over sized mirror in the hallway. Oh wow, I look a mess. My face is all wet and red from the amount of crying. I can't believe Jax held me down on the floor like that. I wanted to tell him in private. Then he could have met Finley, but he made me shout the truth at him instead. In front of everyone! Jax is probably so angry at me that he never wants to see me again. I can't blame him, but I hope he still wants to see Finley. A good bath is what I need, so I make my way upstairs and hope it can calm me down.

After a wonderful hot and steamy bath, that was hot enough to turn my skin red, I do feel a little better. While I was relaxing I ran over everything that had happened yesterday and this morning. I tried to not think of that kiss, but I can't help it. It has planted itself into my brain. Thinking about how Jax took control of my mouth makes my lips tingle. It's like he's just kissed me all over again. No more worrying about getting carried away with Jax. He won't want to be near me after what I've said to him. Never mind him wanting to kiss me again.

I get dressed and leave my hair in its high messy bun that I did before I got into the bath. My phone very loudly vibrates on my dressing table. I'm shocked to see it's a text from Jax.

JAX: I'm sorry x

I start to cry again all over again. I didn't expect that and he shouldn't be saying he's sorry to me. I'm the one in the wrong. I know he was tough on me earlier but that's Jax, and he knew how to get what he wanted out of me.

ME: No, I'm sorry Jax. So sorry I lied to you x

JAX: I shouldn't have pushed U like that. I made U cry. I just wanted 2 help U and if that meant getting a name I just had to get it out of U. Y did U lie to me Kendal? Y didn't U tell me? x

ME: R U still OK 2 come over? x

JAX: On my way x

He's coming over now? Shit I'd better get ready!

I quickly make my face look better. Jax may be angry with me, but there's no need for him to see me in this mess. I make sure the house is presentable and quickly manage to get myself together before there's a loud knock on the door. I take a deep breath and when I open the door I hold back my gasp. Jax looks distraught. His eyes are so sad, and when he walks past me he doesn't carry himself with his usual confidant swagger. How could I have done this to him? I'm a terrible, terrible person!

I quietly shut the door and lead Jax into my living room. When I sit down on the sofa, I see Jax is still standing, looking at the large photo frame hanging on the wall above my other sofa. The large frame holds twenty photos that scatter in different positions. They're a few of me and Finley together, but most of them are just Finley. Jax stands there staring at it, his broad back facing me. I can see he's breathing heavily through his tight top. I start to feel like I can't hold myself together. I can not cry again. I've cried enough today but looking at the man I love, looking like this - has become my undoing, and I feel my tears stroll down my face. I feel so shit that I have done this, I thought I was doing the right thing. Looking at Jax makes me believe I got it all wrong. So totally wrong.

I look down to the floor because I can't handle looking at him anymore. It's too much and it's breaking me. I can't hold my tears back any longer, so I hang my head and try my best to cry silently. I thought I was doing a good job until I see Jax's knees crouch down next to my feet and then his two strong hands hold my head on either side. Jax lifts my face so I look at him crouching down in front of me. The look on his face breaks me again. He looks concerned for me - which is wrong. This is about him and Finley. He wipes my tears away with his thumbs and kisses my forehead.

"Don't cry baby. I'm here now for you. For both of you."

Which just makes me cry harder and he pulls me into his arms. How can he be so good to me? I can't take his kindness, I need him to shout at me or at least look at me with disgust.

"I-I'm s-so sorry Jax."

I manage to say between my sobs. There was no point in me

putting on fresh make-up. Jax holds me tighter and I breathe in his scent. I'm immediately taken back four years, old favourite memories flood back. I loved getting up and close to Jax, wrapped in his large tattooed arms. I breathe him in some more and his smell manages to calm me down, he has always smelt so good.

"Why? I could have helped you. I could have been with you. You shouldn't have done this alone for so long Kendal. You don't know how angry I am right now that you robbed me of this. Not just lying about Finley but I should have been here for you too."

There's no point in lying anymore, so I let it all fall out.

"When I found out I was pregnant I knew I had to keep the baby, but I couldn't take your dream away Jax. You loved playing, and you were getting more and more attention. You were finally getting somewhere; if I had told you I was pregnant with your baby it would have ruined everything for you."

"Don't be so stupid. I could have been there for you both and still have had Decoy."

I pull away from him so I can look him straight in the face.

"No you couldn't!"

He frowns down at me, so I quickly say what I have too.

"When Finley was about a week old, I heard the news you had been signed. Are you telling me you would have left Finley – to go and do the promotional tour when he was that young?"

Jax is now the one to look down at the floor. I know I have him.

"I could have sorted something."

"That's what I didn't want you to do. I wanted you to be happy and live your dream. Not stressing about how to fix it all. I couldn't take that away from you. I originally planned to tell Finley when he was a teenager, but this year has been so hard. I couldn't do it anymore Jax. Finley needs you."

He looks at me and softly strokes my cheek.

"Kendal, I was happy and living my dream when you were with me. When you left I wasn't happy anymore. I wasn't living my dream anymore. Being with you was my dream. Being without you was miserable."

I don't know what to say. Jax lifts one of his eyebrows and smiles. It warms me inside because he looks a little better than ten minutes ago.

"So, you named him Finley?"

I smile back. I always loved the name. When I found out that was also Jax's middle name, I was so happy that if we stayed together and had a family our sons name would be special. Even though we were not together as a family, we still created a son together. I had to call him Finley.

Jax glances back to the wall where the multi photo frame is hung.

"He's a good looking kid."

I giggle. That's because he takes after his dad.

"He's so much like you Jax. In everything. He's your little double."

He turns back to me and my heart drops. He has tears in his eyes.

"Tell me about him, please."

So I do. I tell him everything. I show him old photos and videos on my phone. With every memory I share, every photo and video I show him, he seems to slip back to the same old Jax. Feeding Jax information about his son is putting him back together. I know what I have to do now. After talking and laughing about Finley for an hour, I get a text from my mum. Finley will be here in about fifteen minutes but I don't want Jax to meet my mum yet. That can wait.

"Do you want to meet him?"

He nods and looks back down the photo he's holding. It's a picture of me and Finley in the park, Finley was about nine months old. The photo shows me holding Finley smiling at the camera. It was a windy day, so my red hair is blowing and little Finley's grinning a gummy-toothless smile. It's a beautiful picture. I have it on my phone, so I've given the picture to Jax.

"When Finley comes back. Could you stay upstairs until my mum goes? Then you can come down and meet just Finley."

"OK."

This big, strong, sexy man, who faces big crowds of screaming fans and paparazzi, suddenly seems very nervous. I put my hand on his knee and squeeze.

"It's going to be fine Jax."

~Jax~

Kendal has just spotted her mums car outside, so I've come upstairs to hide away from her. Kendal wants me to meet Finley first and then introduce me to her parents. It makes sense, so I agreed. I just want to meet my son, and after listening to Kendal telling me all about Finley, I'm so nervous to meet him.

Eventually, I got my head around the idea of having a son. Now, the wish I wanted of having my own little family is starting to become a reality. I was still angry with Kendal when I came over here, but when I saw what state she was in, my anger lessoned. She looked so small and fragile. Her little face all red and her eyes were puffy. I knew me making her come clean had done that and I'm disappointed in myself treating her like that. I had no idea she was going to tell me I was Finley's father.

Being angry at Kendal for keeping this secret doesn't change how I feel about her. I'm not angry at her for not telling me I have a son. It's because she left me when she needed me the most and raised our child alone for nearly four years. I'm angry because I've wasted those four years, spending them with pointless women – when I could have had Kendal. Spent time - bonding with my son. I don't know how it would have all worked out. I would have tried everything. Maybe Decoy might not have been where we are today. It might have taken longer to get where we wanted to be, or it might not have happened at all. I wouldn't have cared because I would have had Kendal and Finley.

I wasn't lying when I told her my dream was with her. After Kendal had run out on me, I soon realized that I was not living the dream anymore. Yes, I loved being the front man of Decoy and singing to the fans. Without Kendal with me - the parties were boring and my bed was cold. I wanted

Decoy and Kendal. If I had to make that decision four years ago – Kendal was right. I wouldn't have gone on the promotion tour. I would've told the guys to go on without me. Max could've taken over my place easily. As long as I could have had a few local gigs singing and playing my guitar, I would have been perfectly happy.

I get to the top of the stairs. It's a small square landing; three walls face me in a box design. Each wall has a door. I can tell the room right in front of me is the bathroom and I poke my head into the room on the left. It's obviously Kendal's, it's decorated in red and blacks. I walk around and see she has cute little pictures of her and her friends. The flowers I gave her are on a small table in the corner of her room and the picture I had framed for her is in front of them.

I hear the door open downstairs and the sounds of Kendal talking to her mum. Quietly, I walk out onto the landing so I can hear better. My cue to go downstairs, is when Kendal tells Finley that she has someone she wants him to meet.

When I step onto the landing, I look at the third door. That must be Finley's room. I slowly open the door to another small glimpse of Finley. On the wall facing me is red wallpaper with small black guitars and drum kits scattered around. There are boys toys all over. Not in a mess, but where Finley obviously has his fun. I can tell he loves cars, but when I see the blue toy guitar and microphone with stand in the corner - I feel a little emotional. It's only a toy, but I feel as if it links Finley to me. The sound of a door closing downstairs brings me to attention. I walk back onto the landing.

"I can't wait for the cake mummy."

"You can have it after your dinner Finley."

Holy shit! That's my son's voice. My heart is beating so fast I think it's going to take off. I can't help but smile as I listen to

Finley begging Kendal for the cake.

"Later Finley. First there's somebody I want you to meet."

Shit, that's my cue to get downstairs. I've never been so scared.

On my way down, I see Kendal first because she's standing right at the bottom of the stairs. She smiles and reaches out to hold my hand. I'm grateful because my legs have suddenly gone stiff.

Kendal leads me further into the hallway where I see my little boy. I know straight away he's my son, he looks just like me. Poor guy even has the same messy hair as mine. Kendal leaves me and goes over to Finley. I watch as she crouches down to Finley's eye level. Finley looks at Kendal and then back to me. He tilts his head to one side. This little guy is cute as hell.

"Mummy...That man looks like me."

Smart too. I look at Kendal and she's looking right back at me. Her eyes are all shiny with tears. Finley takes his eyes away from me and back to his mum. I'm not going to lie, that felt weird thinking of Kendal as a mum. It's going to take some time getting used to.

"He looks like you baby because he's your daddy."

Kendal is now crying and Finley looks back to me.

"Jax?"

I nod at him. How does he know my name? And how did he connect my name to his dad? Finley's eyes go wide and his face lights up in excitement.

"Daddy?"

I nod again with a little smile but I can feel my mouth shaking a little. Fuck I can't cry. Finley's going to think I'm a pussy. Suddenly, Finley has his arms out and running towards me. I crouch down in time for him to run straight into my arms. He wraps his little arms around my neck and squeezes.

"Mummy said I would see my daddy soon."

"I'm here buddy."

I hold Finley tight against me. I open my eyes and see Kendal crying her eyes out watching us. Finley pulls back and looks up at me. His eyes roam all over me - from my hair, down my body, all over my tattoos and to my shoes.

"My daddy is the coolest!"

I hear a sound from Kendal – a mixture of a sob and a laugh. I feel proud Finley already thinks I'm cool. He doesn't even know how cool I can be. I've missed four years of his life and I'm going to try my best to make up for that.

Chapter 2

"You're a rock star?"

I nod with a massive grin on my face. Kendal laughs beside me. I love how Finley is looking at me in awe. Just how a boy should look at his dad. We're sat around Kendal's kitchen table eating a pizza that I paid for. Me and Kendal had a little disagreement about who was going to pay. I won!

I've spent all afternoon with Kendal and Finley. Kendal hasn't really said much, just sat back and watched me and Finley. Conversation has moved onto me being in a band because Finley wanted to show me his guitar after the pizza. Kendal told Finley that I had a guitar of my own – so Finley's never ending questions began again.

"Yeah, I'm in a band called Decoy. I sing and play the guitar."

Finley gasps with his mouth wide open. Good job Finley has no food in his mouth.

"Like me daddy!"

I swear every time he calls me daddy my chest puffs out in pride. The way Finley looks at me makes me feel like I'm the best man in the world. I love him so much already it's unreal. Kendal laughs again and takes a bite out of her pizza. How can a woman look sexy eating pizza? I had to hold back a groan of need when I walked into the kitchen before we ate. She had wandered off, leaving me and Finley alone, so I went to find her. When I walked into the kitchen, she was picking up some of Finley's toy off the floor. Her perfect-plump-behind was high in the air.

After spending some hours with Finley, I realised that I love her even more. Not only has she brought my son into the world, but she did it alone. Kendal has raised an awesome little boy, I'm so proud of her. My anger has all gone. Apart from the bit where she left me.

"Mummy? Can I get my guitar?"

"Have you finished your pizza?"

"Yep. All full."

"Then yes you can."

He jumps down from the chair and darts out the room. I see Kendal look at me out the corner of her eye. I rest my arm on the back of her chair and lean in close, so my nose touches the bottom of her ear. I feel her shiver.

"You're a fucking fantastic woman."

Kendal turns to face me. Her eyebrows frowning a little.

"What?"

I look down to her luscious lips and fight not to take them when she runs her tongue along them. Our faces are so close that I could attack them.

"I said you're fucking fantastic Kendal."

Before anything else can be said, Finley shouts from his room.

"DADDDDDDYYYYYY!"

I smile and Kendal giggles. Kendal stands and walks to the bottom of the stairs.

"What's the matter Fin?"

There's just silence. Me and Kendal look at each other through the doorway and wait for a reply.

"No, I need my daddy."

Kendal huffs and walks back into the kitchen. She has a smile on her face as she picks up the takeaway boxes.

"Your son needs you Jax."

I still can't believe all of this. It's unreal, but I get up and walk towards the stairs with a big stupid smile on my face.

When I pass Kendal, I let my hand innocently glide across her bum-cheek softy. I feel Kendal freeze and hold back a laugh.

What I see when I go into Finley's bedroom - makes my smile widen. He has his guitar under one arm and holding a microphone, whilst trying to keep a hold of the microphone stand too. The poor guy.

"I need help daddy."

I take everything off him, hold the toys under one arm and lift Finley in the other.

"Wow daddy, you're strong!"

My life has definitely changed for the better.

~Kendal~

I watch Jax run up the stairs to help Finley. It was so cute when Finley asked for Jax and the excited look on Jax's face was adorable. Having him around the house hasn't been weird at all. In fact it's felt quite nice. Finley hasn't found it all weird at all; he has taken to Jax so well. Like he's always had Jax in his life, which is good for everyone.

I'm putting plates into the sink when I hear Finley's laughter. I turn around and my heart leaps out my chest for two completely different reasons. One reason is because Jax is holding the toys under one arm and Finley under the other. His muscles are bulging through his top. Wow, he looks so good in that tight white shirt!

The other reason is because Finley looks so happy and Jax is looking down at him with the same smile. Jax sets the toys down and adjusts Finley so he's holding him upright.

"Jax don't move."

I grab my phone and snap a picture of them both smiling at me. I look at the picture and feel all kinds of emotions. Their first picture as father and son.

"You OK mummy?"

I look up from the picture and to Jax and Finley. Jax sets Finley down and picks up his toys.

"Come on buddy, how about you set up and wait for me and your mum OK?"

Finley nods and follows Jax into the living room. As soon as I'm alone I feel my tears. I'm sick to death of crying all the time! Before I can wipe them away Jax reappears in the kitchen.

"Kendal?"

"I'm fine."

"No you're not. What's wrong?"

I can hear Finley playing his guitar and singing loudly.

"I feel like shit. You two are perfect together. You should have had years of this, not a couple of hours."

He takes me into his arms and holds the back of my head so I can't escape.

"I'm happy Kendal. Now come on, our son is waiting to perform."

That whole sentence felt bizarre. It's going to take some getting used too.

"You're loving the fact Finley thinks your a God, aren't you?"

He holds me at arms length and beams the totally charming Jax Parker smile. I admit. I swoon.

"A God huh?"

My damn cheeks burn. Jax just laughs at me and holds my hand as we walk into the living room - where Finley is waiting excitedly. We both take our seats on the sofa, Jax sits very close, one of his arms goes around my back and his hand rests on the top of my thigh. Very smooth Jax! When I give him a questioning look, he just lifts an eyebrow in a sexy manor. That's right, even Jax's eyebrows are sexy! Finley starts jumping around and shouting. He's totally oblivious to the change of atmosphere between me and Jax.

~*~*~

An hour later, Finley's very loud performance has ended

and it was time to settle him down. Jax had a glimpse into his certain stubbornness in his wardrobe area. Yes, he still has total control when he selects his pajamas. Jax had a lot of fun tormenting Finley with his pajamas, mixing them up, nearly causing Finley's head to explode.

Now I'm listening into Jax reading Finley his bedtime story. I thought I would feel a little jealous of Jax reading to him, but I'm pleased to say that I don't. Listening to Jax reading - has made me so happy. There were some nights after I had read to Finley and he had fallen asleep, that I would think about Jax. I would think about where he was and what he was doing. Other times I wondered if he would've loved Finley's bedtime routine as much as me. By the enthusiasm Jax is putting into reading the book, I would say he does.

I take a quick peek and see Jax is laying next to Finley on his bed, with his head angled up on the headboard. Finley's little head is peaking over his quilt, resting on the crook of Jax's arm that is behind his head - with his eyes closed. Jax looks up at me and winks. I feel so guilty not telling him sooner. Finley should have had Jax in his life a lot sooner.

I leave Jax to it and creep downstairs. I sit in the living room and check my phone. I have a few messages from the girls to see if I'm OK.

Five minutes later Jax returns from Finley's room looking very happy with himself.

"I didn't think I would enjoy that so much."

I know exactly what he means. As a parent it's a wonderful feeling reading as your child falls asleep. Giving them that kiss on their forehead and tucking them in.

"I know."

He comes to sit beside me.

"Thanks Kendal. Today's been fantastic. Finley's an awesome kid."

"It's OK. He's loved today as much as you have. He will be sad to see you gone in the morning."

Shit, I shouldn't have said that! It makes it sound like I want him to stay. Well, I do, but he doesn't need to know that. Jax looks at me and smiles a little. It's not a happy smile. I've upset him.

"Sorry, I shouldn't have said that."

"No, it's just….I was wondering, when can I see him again?"

"Well, he has school tomorrow. You can come with me to pick him up if you like?"

His smile is back and I'm relieved.

"That's great. Where shall I meet you?"

We agree to meet at my work so Jax can follow me there. I finish at 3:00 tomorrow, just in time to be able to fetch Finley. We start to laugh about old times; I fall back against the back of the sofa laughing so hard. Jax is still sitting forward looking at me with a heated look. I'd know that look anywhere. It does delicious things to my body and my stomach tightens in anticipation.

"You don't know how many times I thought about seeing you again."

"You did?"

He nods and leans in a little closer. Oh my, can I kiss him again? I lick my lips and his eyes watch my tongue.

"I thought a lot about you too."

"Did you now?"

He flashes that cocky grin at me before he closes the space between us, and he kisses me with enough passion to light a fire. His tongue demands attention from mine. I hear myself sigh, Jax feels so good. He pushes me to lie down on the sofa and Jax falls on top, supporting his weight with his arms. How many times have I fantasied about this over the last four years? Too many times!

I grab onto either side of his face and deepen the kiss; his grunt of approval pushes me on to let my hands wander over his muscled body. I grab onto his tight arse and Jax presses his groin into me, I groan in need. The last time I had sex was with Harley, over six months ago. When I feel Jax's hard cock against me, I pull down on his arse to make his hardness press into me more. Jax trails his kisses onto my jaw and neck, it feels so good. I need more. Jax whispers against my skin.

"I've missed you so bad baby."

"Me too."

I grab his face again and pull him back to my lonely mouth. I'm about to demand that Jax end's my burning need – when there is a knock on the front door.

"You expecting anyone?"

I shake my head but I can't ignore it. I get up on my shaky legs and gather myself together. I walk to my door with Jax behind me. I'm surprised to see its Jessica with Sam standing behind her - looking like he really doesn't want to be here.

"So, I came here to check in on you seeing as I've had no replies to my texts."

"I was busy Jess."

She glances at Jax behind me and quirks an eyebrow.

"I came to check on you because last time you were together you were crying on the floor, but it looks to me like you're getting on just fine."

I bite my lip and try to think what to say, but Jax steps closer and wraps his arms around me from behind.

"Hey Jess, Sam."

Sam and Jax do the man head nod.

"Sorry Kendal, I tried to stop her coming over."

Yeah I bet he did, but Jessica's the type of girl that when she's on a mission - nobody can stop her. Not even Sam. They say their goodbyes and leave.

"I should probably get going too."

"Oh OK."

Damn. I wanted to finish what' we'd started. Jax gives me a strong armed cuddle and I relax into him.

"Thank you for today baby. I'm gonna be by your side from now on. You can't get rid of me now."

"I wouldn't want too."

I mean it. Seeing Jax and Finley today has made me see they need each other. Jax probably needs Finley more than Finley needs Jax to be honest.

"What time do you leave tomorrow?"

"Half past eight. Why?"

"You better get some sleep then. I'll see you tomorrow."

He gives me a kiss on my mouth and I lean into him, wanting more. Jax leans away chuckling, the bastard knows what he's doing to me.

He gives me one last peck on my mouth before he leaves and gets into his flashy car. I shut the door and hear the roar of the engine as he drives away. Leaving me very unsatisfied.

Chapter 3

When my alarm woke me the next morning I was shocked. That hasn't happened for about two years!

Where is Finley?

I sit up in my bed and look around. As if I'm going to find my son on my bedroom floor or something. I get out of my bed and tip toe over to Finley's room, just in case he's still sleeping.

When I see him sitting on his bed my heart breaks. Finley has his legs crossed with the toy guitar on his lap. His head is bowed down and he keeps flicking the pretend guitar strings. Finley looks so sad it makes me want to cry. I slowly walk into his room but he doesn't even look up.

"Finley?"

His head slowly looks up to me and he catches my breath. He's been crying! And I've been sleeping! I quickly walk and sit beside him on the bed. My arms wrap around him and I smooth his hair with my hand.

"What's the matter Finley?"

He snuffles a little so I give him a little kiss on top of his hair.

"My daddy is gone."

Oh my god! My poor little baby boy. He thinks Jax has gone for good. I won't let that happen. Now that they have found each other they will never lose one another. That's my mission for keeping them apart for nearly four years. I scoot away from Finley a little and place my hands on either side of his face.

"No baby he's not gone."

"I went downstairs and daddy gone mummy."

His voice breaks and he rubs his eyes.

"Daddy has gone home to sleep. He has a house with his friends honey. Daddy will be here again when you finish school."

Immediately his tears are gone and he smiles a little weak grin at me.

"Really?"

"Yes. Your daddy is not going away again Finley. He will always want to see you. OK?"

He nods and gives me a cuddle. Maybe I should have explained this to Finley before he went to sleep last night. After all, he did go to sleep while Jax was still here. He was bound to think he would still be here when he woke up.

After breakfast and a few cartoons Finley seems back to himself now.

When I text Jax to tell him what Finley had said this morning he rang me straight away worrying about Finley. They spoke on the phone and ever since Finley has been his usual chirpy self. He's going to be a daddy's boy I know it. I knew he would.

I shout for Finley to come upstairs when I'm ready for work so he can get dressed for school. When I've spiked his hair a little he frowns up at me.

"Why don't daddy live in our house?"

What can I say?

"Erm. Well, Finley, it's because....."

"Logans daddy lives with him and his mummy. And they have a baby. If daddy lives with us will we have a baby? I want a baby mummy."

Oh fucking hell. One thing at a time Finley.

"Logans mummy and daddy live together because they're boyfriend and girlfriend."

"EEERRRRR."

I laugh. Give it twelve years or so Finley, then you won't think the idea of girlfriends and kissing is disgusting.

"So if daddy lives here. Daddy would be your boyfriend?"

"Erm. Yes Finley bu-"

"You need to be daddy's girlfriend mummy. So daddy can live here and we can all have a baby."

"What? Finley that's not-"

"I want a sister mummy. Not a brother."

Oh dear Lord what the hell are we talking about?

I manage to take the topic away from babies to Finley's birthday. He wants a party and of course now I have to invite Jax. I wonder how the guests are going to deal with Finley's dad being a rock star. No doubt Rhys, Leo and Max will want to come too. Imagine that article in the paper, hilarious.

When it's 08:25 Finley and I are all ready to leave. I manage to fit in a quick morning cup of tea when there's a knock on the door. What the hell, who can that be?

Nobody comes by in the morning, unless the postman is delivering a package. But I'm not expecting anything today. Finley doesn't move from the TV, he probably hasn't even heard the door.

I'm shocked when I unlock and open the door.

"Jax?"

Standing there looking totally fucking sexy is Jax with a smirk on his face.

"What are you doing here?"

He leans in and gives me a long kiss on the lips. I don't realise that I'm moaning against him until he laughs. I guess I'm still a little sensitive from last night. Those lips of his can work wonders and last night whilst I was lying alone in my bed I ran through all the memories I had stored away.

Jax steps into the hallway while I just stare at him. Why is he here? I told him we leave at this time.

"I decided I wanted to see my little man before he went to school."

On Jax talking Finley had snapped out his cartoon daze and ran out the living room.

"Daddddyyyy!"

Finley runs right up to Jax and grabs his legs. Jax reaches

down and lifts him into a hug. I listen as Jax reassures Finley that he's not going anywhere and he will always be with Finley. I can't help but think about what will happen when Jax goes away on tour again. I'm going to be left with a heartbroken Finley. To tell you the truth, I will be sad to see him leave too, it's weird how fast I'm getting used to seeing Jax again. I'm hoping Finley doesn't start talking about Jax moving in and having a little sister. That would be a little awkward.

~Jax~

I already secretly planned to come back here this morning but the look on Kendal's face is fucking priceless. Yesterday was one of the best days in my life, if not **the** best.

Last night with Kendal was pretty amazing too and I'm glad Jessica came knocking when she did. As much as I would have loved to have had my way with Kendal last night I couldn't. I need to do this the right way. Today is the first step in getting to know my son more, getting Kendal back and therefore having my family. There were times when I daydreamed about still being with Kendal and starting a family and my wish has come true. Kendal doesn't realize but this was my dream. The band, Kendal and us. Having a family and making us permanent.

This morning I wanted to surprise Kendal. The look on her face assures me I have. My son is bouncing in my arms. I look at Finley, my perfect little boy. How many times I imagined what my son would look like, if I had one. Here he is, my little mini me. When Kendal text me earlier telling me what had happened this morning my decision to come back here was final. I won't let him think I'm not here for him.

Finley is beaming a huge smile at me.

"Mummy said I can have a party."

A party? Does he mean a birthday party? Kendal said he was nearly four but I didn't think so soon. Shit, I should have asked when his birthday is last night.

"A party? You're a lucky boy."

I see it's now 08:35 and I know Kendal likes to keep to a time limit. That was always her thing. She hates being late. Kendal is still standing by the open door, silent but smiling at me and Finley.

"Don't you have to get going?"

"Sorry, I didn't want to disturb you two. You look cute together."

She has a little shine in her eyes and I know she's feeling emotional again.

"We have to take this little man to school then."

"We?"

"Well now I'm here I might as well come with you."

She doesn't need to know I came here for that reason. When I asked her what time she usually leaves in the morning, I knew what I was going to do.

"Erm, OK. Fin come and choose your shoes."

Kendal told me Finley has a certain way with his clothes and shoes and I think it's hilarious. It's only natural my son would have swag. He's three and he knows what clothes he likes and how to wear them. He's one cool kid. I watch as he takes his black high top Converse to Kendal.

Today Finley has long style denim shorts on and a black t-shirt with white skulls on. When he has his shoes tied onto his feet, he dashes upstairs shouting he's forgotten something. Kendal laughs as she grabs her bag and puts on her shoes. She's looking super sexy today in her work uniform. I'm so glad no guys go into her work place because I know they would be fucking all over her.

Finley comes running back down the stairs and I see he now has a black flat peek hat on. On the front is a white star and under the peek is white, this kid has some serious swagger. He looks cool as fuck, better than me actually.

"Wow Finley, you look like a rock star."

"I know because you are."

"He asked me this morning to see pictures of you. So I searched you on the internet."

I cringe. I hope he didn't see the bad ones. Kendal leans close as she walks by me.

"Don't worry, I made sure he only saw certain ones."

Thank fuck for that.

"Yeah daddy. I wanted to see what you wear."

This kid makes me feel like the best fucking man alive more and more.

"I saw the pictures of you and mummy. Will I be in pictures?"

Oh shit. Me and Kendal share a glance. I hadn't thought of the press getting their greedy hands on information about Finley. Lucky I sorted Kendal so they will think she's a long time girlfriend but I need to protect Finley. I won't let him be hurt and I don't want him harassed. Me and Kendal need to talk about this and I need to ring Angie, my Media manager who deals with all this shit.

Kendal reaches for her car keys from the bowl on the kitchen counter and I walk quickly by her side and take her keys from her. She gawps at me and frowns a little.

"Jax what are you doing?"

"I told you, we're taking Finley school."

"Yes but I need my keys to drive."

"Nope. You're coming in my car."

"No I'm not. I need to get to work."

"I know. We're taking Finley to school then I will take you to work."

She rolls her eyes and tries to reach for her keys but I hold them high so she can't reach. I hear Finley giggling.

"Jax come on."

"No, I'm taking you and I'm picking you up from work."

Kendal is now frowning at me. Is it weird that I'm strangely turned on by this?

"You can't take me to and from work. That's ridiculous."

"Call it what you like but it's happening."

I put her keys in the inside pocket of my leather jacket and walk by her.

"I'd hurry if I were you."

I catch a glance of her panicked look when she realizes the time. I try and hold in my smile because I know I'll get my own way. I know how to work Kendal and it feels so fucking good to have her back. Hopefully it won't be too long until she's 100% completely mine. Finley's jumping around in the hallway.

"Yay! Going school in daddy's car!"

Every time I hear Finley call me daddy makes me feel happier than the last. How could my fantasy finally come true?

When me and Finley walk out the house hand in hand I hear Kendal behind me huffing as she locks up her house and gets Finley's car seat. A wild thought pops up when Kendal finally drops herself heavily onto the seat next to me.

"What are you smiling about Jax?"

I can't tell her what I'm really thinking. She will freak out.

"Nothing baby. Now tell me where the little rock stars school is."

Kendal guides me to Finley's school. I'm impressed. Not by what the school looks like, I knew Kendal would choose a good school for our son. It's the fact it's a very private looking building. High fences covered in green shrubbery surround the school so that you can't see through. The front gates are open but Kendal tells me they only open five minutes before you collect the children and the only people who can pick up a child are the people that are listed. I'm pleased with this for security reasons for Finley, seeing as he probably will have his media debut some time soon. Maybe we need to move him to a school that's more experienced with celebrity kids. Is there even such a place?

I'm surprised how emotional this whole first school drop of

is. Finley introduces me to all his little friends.

I notice some parents who take in who I really am. They probably didn't think that a rock star would be at a school at 9:00 in the morning. Kendal is off talking to a teacher while I watch Finley walk around his classroom. My kid is seriously fucking cool. He walks around his class with two boys following him everywhere. Little girls taunt him and I see Finley getting annoyed. I can't help but smile thinking about his years to come. His annoyance with girls will only progress as he gets older, only for a whole different reason.

We say our goodbyes to Finley, who gives both me and Kendal huge hugs and wet kisses. When we get back into the car Kendal huffs.

"Did you have to bring this flashy thing?"

"Why what's wrong?"

"Everyone's staring. Look all the men are looking."

I would like to say that all the men, teachers and parents, are looking at my car. But they're not. I didn't miss the fact that men seem to follow Kendal with their eyes. They always have, but over the years Kendal has blossomed into a beautiful and confidant woman. She oozes sex appeal.

"Come on woman. They're not all looking at the car."

"Oh don't be big headed Mr Rock star."

She rolls her eyes at me. Is she really that oblivious to what she looks like? Especially when she's in her sexy little work uniform. I'd love to take her one day while she's wearing that.

"They weren't looking at me either. Kendal do you not know you're a MILF?"

"What?"

"MILF. You know. Mother I'd-"

"Yes I know what it means and you can stop."

I see she's blushing. I love making her blush. I wonder if her little pussy still gets red when I've had my way with it for so long?

"I spoke to Finley's teacher. I've added you to his list. So if you want to pick him up, you can."

I'm taken by surprise. She did that? I can pick him up? Take him out?

"Thanks Kendal."

She gives me her sweetest smile.

"It's the least I can do Jax."

"You can stop that now Kendal."

She frowns and looks down at her handbag.

"What?"

"Stop feeling guilty. It's done now. Forgotten. I'll forget if you will."

"How can you forgive me?"

"Easy. I've missed four years of this. I'm not wasting anymore time. I'm just going to enjoy everything. That means you can stop with those sad eyes and leaving me and Finley alone any chance you get."

She bites down so hard on her lip that I think it's going to bleed.

"Yeah don't think I didn't notice that yesterday."

I tug her bottom lip out from the torture of her tooth with my thumb and kiss it better. When I open my eyes Kendal has hers closed.

"Right lets get you to work."

Chapter 4

~Kendal~

I can't believe Jax is driving me to work. As soon as he pulls up outside work the girls will all be gawping.

"I was thinking, is it OK to buy something for Finley?"

I look to Jax and he's staring out at the road while he's driving. I take advantage of taking in the male beauty next to me.

"Jax you can do anything you want but you don't have to buy him stuff. Save your money and wait until his birthday."

Jax laughs a little and I realize what I've just said. Stupid Kendal. Jax isn't worried about spending too much money. I'm a fucking idiot.

"I want to surprise him when he gets back from school."

That seems sweet enough. I can't tell the man no. Even if I did he would just do it anyway.

"You don't have to ask my permission Jax. Finley is your son too."

He gives me the sexiest smile and I'm glad I'm sat down because it's one of those smiles that makes your legs wobble. How dare he flash me his sexy smile. He knows what that does to me, well he used to.

When he pulls up outside my work he runs around and opens my door. He holds my hand as I get out which makes me giggle and I hear the click of a camera. Jax turns around and sure enough there's three chubby guys with cameras.

"Come on lets get you inside."

Jax holds my hand as we quickly walk into the salon. When we walk in it's dead quiet which is unusual. I know it's because Jax is here. He ignores the silence and grabs my face with his hands and leans in for a kiss.

"Tonight we need to talk."

"We do?"

"I need to tell you what I told my media manager about you for the press. We also need to think about Finley."

I agree, what he said this morning about him being in pictures worried me.

"OK."

He gives me that sexy smile again and I prepare my legs. He gives me another quick kiss and walks outside to his car. Completely happy with himself. What the hell is happening? And why is he talking to his media manager about me for press? That's not necessary.

As soon as I step further into the salon Tanya marches up to me, grabs hold of my wrist and doesn't let go until we get into the staff room. Everyone's getting their tables ready for the day so it's empty.

"What is going on with you two?"

"What do you mean?"

"Yesterday he had you screaming and crying. Now he's dropping you off at work with a sloppy goodbye kiss. You look like a couple for Christ sake. What has happened since you left Sophies yesterday? All I got was a text telling me you're fine late last night. I knew I should have come over."

"He came by yesterday and we spoke for hours. We talked about everything. He asked about Finley and I let him meet him. They're perfect together Tan, Finley adores him."

She huffs and puts her hands on her hips.

"Well OK, that sounds fair enough but why was he here this morning?"

Her eyes widen.

"Oh my God! You didn't?"

"What? No!"

I quickly explain why he was over this morning. Although I have a sneaky feeling he was going to come over before I had even told him about Finley crying. Then I realize, Jax still has my car keys.

After I've stopped talking Tanya's face has softened a little but her hands are still on those hips of hers.

"I like the man and everything Kendal but what he did yesterday I will never forget. I hope you know I gave him a piece of my mind when you ran out."

I would think so. If she didn't she wouldn't be the Tanya I know.

"Are you getting back together?"

"No. He just wants to spend time with Finley."

"But you love him."

I nod at her. Of course I love him but I don't think I should let my feelings enter this whole mess. It will make it a lot harder when I'm around Jax. I'm going to have to tell him to stop the kisses because I can't concentrate when those lips are on mine. After Finley's words this morning, I don't want him getting the wrong idea about us.

As I'm putting my bag away safely into my locker I feel my phone vibrate. I'm thinking it might be Jax but it's my mum.

MUM: What R U doing 4 UR dinner today? We need 2 talk x

Oh dear. That doesn't sound so good. Better to get this over with but shit I don't have my car. Fucking Jax.

ME: I'm free but I didn't drive to work today. I need a lift x

MUM: Y? UR dad will B there. What time? x

ME: Ill explain later. 12 please x

MUM: UR dad will B there. Love U x

ME: Love you x

I set my phone back in my bag and lock it away.

"Who was that?"

"Mum, wants me over for dinner."

"Cool. Can I tag along?"

I wish.

"I'd love you to but I think it's going to be an intense conversation. I need to tell them everything."

Tanya grimaces and then starts laughing.

"Good luck."

Oh thanks.

~Jax~

As soon as I left Kendal I rang our media manager, Angie. I need to have this woman on fucking speed dial now. I have to protect Finley, I saw Kendal's face when he mentioned getting photographed.

Basically the whole story that will be fed to the media, when they find out for themselves, is that me and Kendal have been on and off since we were eighteen. She got pregnant when we got signed but we won't say anything about Kendal keeping me in the dark. What will be said though is that when Finley was about four months old we separated because the band was everywhere and we never saw each other. I decided I wanted to keep them a secret so they didn't get attention. I didn't want them hounded, I wanted my son to have a normal life. The media will think I kept in touch with them, that I saw Finley whenever I had the chance. Throughout the last four years we will tell them that me and Kendal tried to give it another shot but because the band have always been mad crazy, we never had the chance.

Now as a band, we've all decided we need to slow our schedule down a bit. After four years living from a tour bus we want to only have one tour a year rather than tour all year, every year. We've been non stop, so now we want to chill a bit and I'm glad we did because now I have Finley and

I want to be very included in his life.

I will tell the press we no longer see the need to keep Finley a secret so he can spend more time with me. There was no way I was going to get to spend as much time with Finley as I want without paparazzi getting a picture. So hopefully that keeps everyone safe.

Now I'm wishing I had a bigger car to put the presents I bought Finley in. I have a huge box for his trampoline, a wide box for his tent and another long and wide box for his scalextric racetrack. I hope Kendal doesn't get mad at me, not just for buying him stuff but because they aren't exactly small. They're all pretty big. Now I'm off to buy my huge surprise for all three of us. Fingers crossed Kendal won't freak out when I get to show her.

~~*

I walk out the building with a huge smile on my face. How much my life has changed in a week is unbelievable but I fucking love it. That present won't be ready for a month but I can't wait. By that time I'm hoping to have won Kendal back anyway. I have an hour until I need to pick Kendal up from work. I know she's doing what she loves but I wish she was the boss so she could choose her hours and spend more time with me. I know that's selfish but when it comes to that woman, I don't give two shits.

When I get back home Leo and Max are here.

"Where the fuck have you been?"

"Been locked up in Kendal's room already?"

I tell them about my day and they think me keeping Kendal's car keys is hilarious. Leo looks a little uncomfortable.

"Did you get Tanya's number?"

Aw shit, I haven't even asked Kendal.

"I'll ask Kendal tonight. I'm not promising anything."

He nods and stays quiet. Weird. Max has a big smile on his face.

"So what's Finley like?"

I didn't see them when I got in last night which I was pleased about. I had to run straight into a cold shower to cool off the effects from Kendal. I feel my face smile back at Max.

"Fucking hell man he's the coolest kid I've met."

I don't stop talking about him but Leo and Max don't look bothered. They look interested and ask me more questions. Probably because they love Kendal.

"Have you got any pictures?"

Fucking hell I forgot. I show them all the ones Kendal sent from her phone to mine and then I get the picture from my inside pocket. The one that Kendal gave me. I fucking love this picture. Max takes it and smiles.

"She looks happy."

"Yeah, as soon as Finley walks into the room she smiles. He makes her happy and I know why. I feel the same."

I don't care if I sound like a pussy. I'm talking about my son for fuck sake. I'll talk like a pussy as much as I want. Leo is still flicking through the pictures on my phone.

"Fucking hell man. Jax he looks just like you."

"I know, when you see him it's unreal."

Leo and Max both look up at me.

"When will we get to see him?"

I stand up because it's time for me to go pick up my girl.

"I dunno. I'll ask Kendal. He has school all week."

When I leave I don't miss the sad look on Leo's face. What is up with the man?

Chapter 5

~Kendal~

It's nearly 3:00 and I'm on my last customer. It's just a normal standard cut so it won't be long until it's time for me to go home. That means it's closer to when I see Jax again.

The dinner at my parents wasn't so bad. I thought I'd be told off and shouted at like I was a kid again but they were surprisingly OK with everything. I explained everything that had happened and why I kept Jax out of it and they totally understood. I regret not telling them sooner but then again my dad said no man should be kept away from his child, so he most likely would have tracked Jax down himself.

He also revealed he was relieved he didn't have to kick some guy's ass for deserting his daughter and grandson. It was all my fault, so instead of me getting the ass kicking – I got his stern eyes which are worse. Believe me. My mum was a little upset that I didn't tell her but everything's great now. I'm really happy with everything in my life at the minute and it's really weird to not worry and to not have that stabbing of guilt whenever I think about Jax.

As I'm checking to see the girl's hair is all even, I notice she's on a gossip website on her phone. The main picture is a new one of me and Jax at the park. The guy must have been taking photos sooner than when we spotted him because this one is a photo of us walking to the car. We're looking at each other while we're talking and have stupid smiles on our faces. The caption above the photo says.

Could This Girl Be The One?

Jax probably couldn't have a serious relationship anymore. How could he keep to one girl when he has thousands of others throwing themselves at him wherever he goes? I feel guilty for thinking that because Rhys and Sophie seem to be happy enough and I know Rhys is unconditionally in love with Sophie. If only I found a man like that. Sophie is beautiful so Rhys wouldn't even think to look at another girl, but me? Well, I'm just normal looking girl. Other girls would outshine me and take Jax's attention away.

I look at the girl's reflection in the mirror and she's looking back at me. She looks down at her phone then back up. Oh great – she knows that's me in the photo. Especially seeing as I have my work clothes on in the photo, it makes it a little easier for her!

The girl opens her mouth to speak but I just nod and smile before she can ask. She gives me a little excited look and I fight the urge to roll my eyes. I hope I don't have to put up with this anymore, this could disrupt my work.

Fifteen minutes later, the gushing girl has gone – after Bianca had taken a photo of me and the girl and I signed her receipt! I'm now standing outside waiting for Jax to collect me, because he still has my keys. Honestly, I don't understand why I've had this attention from two girls now. It's not me that's famous, it's Jax. No wonder Sophie has kept her identity a secret for all these years. Although, if me and Sophie are always hanging out and now I have some attention from being linked to Jax, won't Sophie get noticed too?

My thoughts are cut short when I hear my name being shouted. I turn my and see Harley walking towards me. Oh shit! I didn't text him back after he'd text me that slightly nasty text about going to dinner with Jax.

Harley stops right in front of me looking as good as ever. He's a very good looking man but now that I've been spending time with Jax again lately, I don't seem to find him as appealing. Don't get me wrong, the way he's looking at me right now makes me feel a little heated, but Jax has damaged me again.

"Hey Kendal."

"Hi."

"Look, I just wanted to say sorry about that text. I was an idiot. I guess I was just jealous."

Jealous? Me and Harley haven't been together for a while now. Why would he still get jealous?

"Jealous?"

"Well yeah. There's no competition between me and a stinking rich rock star."

So he thinks I was with Jax for his money. That makes me pissed.

"I'm not into his money Harley! I've known Jax for six years."

He lifts an eyebrow at me and I feel like punching him in his handsome face.

"You've never spoken about him before."

Well why would I?

"Anyway, why would I choose? We're not dating and neither are me and Jax."

He steps closer to me and I step back towards the wall.

"That's good news I suppose. So, do you wanna go to dinner this weekend? Catch up?"

Seriously? After all that, he tries to put on the moves and ask me out to dinner?

"I don't know Harley."

He frowns down at me and I hear an engine roar from the distance. I want it to be Jax so I can get away from Harley but then if Jax sees Harley this close, I don't want him to get the wrong idea. Harley steps even closer.

"So you will go out with him and not me? I need you back Kendal."

Harley raises his hand to rest on my shoulder and the engine gets louder.

"Harley I've already told you I can't."

He doesn't say anything and I hear the slamming of a door. I can't see because Harley is blocking my vision but I have a feeling I know who it is.

"Kendal?"

I was right. It's Jax and I don't know whether I'm happy or not that he's here while Harley is too. Harley tenses and turns around. Jax frowns at Harley and steps closer to me. Jax finally looks at me and he doesn't look happy.

"Who's this?"

My mouth is dry and I don't think I can speak but Harley decides to talk instead.

"I'm her ex, Harley."

I see Jax tense and all I can think is *fuck fuck fuck!* Harley looks back to me and smiles. He still has that hand on my fucking shoulder so I shake it off.

"So, is that a yes to this weekend?"

What? Has Harley lost his mind? Oh no he's not one of those scary ex stalkers is he? Just my fucking luck.

"This weekend?"

I look back to Jax but he's looking at Harley.

"Yeah, for dinner."

I finally find my voice.

"I didn't say yes."

"Just text me."

And off he goes, leaving me shocked. I don't know what to do or what to say. Harley has always seemed so nice but that wasn't nice at all. That was scary-weird and I didn't like it. Jax takes hold of my hand.

"Kendal?"

I look to him and snap out my weird daze of watching Harley.

"Mmmmm?"

"What was all that about?"

"Nothing, he keeps asking me out. That's all."

"Is he bugging you?"

"No. That just seemed weird."

"Come on."

He pulls me along to the car. When Jax shuts the door behind me, I lean my head back against the headrest. I breathe a huge sigh, that shit was tense! Jax drops down in his seat and looks over at me before he drives.

"If he's bugging you, I'll get rid of him."

What, is Jax in the mafia now? I hold back my laugh and look at him. He looks worried and I can understand. Harley was acting really strange.

"No it's fine. He's a good guy."

I just don't think he gets that I'm not interested, but I keep that thought to myself.

~*~*~

I was OK by the time we got to Finley's school. Finley was overly excited to see Jax and loved the shoulder ride he got to the car. He beamed a smile, looking very proud to be on his daddy's shoulders. I took a picture of them both when we got to the car. The look of them like that – with their identical smiles, was just too adorable to forget.

Now we're at home and Jax showed Finley the gifts he'd got him. The look on Jax's face was adorable as he watched Finley rip them open.

I look at Jax and Finley; they're outside looking at all the scattered pieces to the trampoline.

"Daddy what about this one?"

"Erm, I think daddy needs some help."

He strolls up to me and gets his phone out.

"Is it OK if I ask Leo and Max over? I can't do that thing by myself."

I have no problem with Finley meeting Max and Leo.

"Make sure they're on their best behaviour."

He grins and types a text.

"Oh, I forgot to ask."

He puts his phone away into his back pocket.

"Leo asked if he could have Tanya's number."

"Really?"

I decide to text Tanya because she's at work and she can get back to me whenever she can. Jax said Max and Leo are excited to come over. They sometimes act like kids so I can imagine them getting on really well with Finley.

Only ten minutes later they knock on the door. Max and Leo are stood looking a little weird. Are they nervous? So cute. They each give me a kiss on the cheek and a hug before they walk in.

"Nice place Kendal."

I roll my eyes. Yes my little house might be nice but it will be nothing compared to their place. They're just being nice.

"Yeah yeah."

I go to walk in the garden and Max grabs my arm. Leo stops with us.

"I'm sorry about the other day Kenny."

"It's all forgotten Max."

He smiles sadly and then Leo places his hands on my shoulders.

"Where is this mini Jax then?"

"He told you?"

Max shakes his head.

"Shown us pictures."

I smile as I imagine a happy Jax showing off photos of his son.

"Whoa! Cool daddy!"

Finley shouts from his bedroom. Jax decided to put the Disney Cars tent up in Finley's bedroom while he waited for his helpers. Max and Leo look up the stairs.

"Jax, the guys are here!"

Max smirks at me.

"It's like you're a married couple already."

I bite my lip instead of answering that. Jax comes down the stairs holding Finley over his shoulder who is giggling.

"Hey guys."

He sets Finley down and Max and Leo have their first proper look at him. I see their eyes widen a little at the sight of him. He really does look that much like Jax, even more so – because Jax and Finley are standing side by side.

"Finley, these are my two best friends Max and Leo."

Finley smiles and then bumps fists with them. He giggles some more and then looks to me, his smile still firmly on his face.

"Daddy said that's cool man handshake."

Of course he did. Leo crouches down in front of Finley.

"Hey little man. You look like your daddy."

Finley seems to really like that statement and laughs at Leo. We all go to the back garden, where the trampoline still lays in pieces on the grass. The guys soon get to work and it's not long until there's a big trampoline with it's enclosure on my garden. Finley jumps straight on. With every jump he laughs, I think he may like this more than the play center at my parents. Max can't help himself and gets on with Finley.

All afternoon Finley enjoys himself with his daddy, Max and Leo. At one point I get on the trampoline with Finley and we can't stop laughing. I look over to the guys who are watching and they all had weird looks on their faces. It was a little weird when Jax decided to get on with us. I was also scared the trampoline would break, but it turned out Jax wanted pictures of the three of us together. It wasn't long until the weirdness disappeared and I was laughing as loud as Finley. Finley gets on great with Max and Leo. I can see what Jax meant about Leo acting weird.

Tanya did finally text me back. Her message said she didn't want Leo to have her number. I watched his face fall as I told him what she'd said. It made me feel like shit. I hope these two can sort out whatever is happening between them. I love them both and seeing them like this isn't nice at all.

After a takeaway dinner it was time for Finley to go to bed and he wanted Jax to read him his story. I told Jax to remind him that he won't be here in the morning. I don't want to see Finley like that again.

When Jax and Finley are upstairs, it's just me, Max and Leo. They're helping me tidy up the garden and kitchen from the mad afternoon. We have a laugh as they poke fun at me all the while. They talk about how much of a cool kid Finley is, which makes me proud. When they leave Max gives me a long hug.

"He's been so down lately. You and Finley have made him so happy Kendal. Thank you."

"You shouldn't be saying thank you to me."

"It doesn't matter now Kenny. It's all forgotten."

I watch them get into Max's car. Could everyone really just forgive me like they are? I don't forgive myself.

Chapter 6

~Jax~

I lay Finley down on his bed and sit down beside him. He picked a story but before I start to read, I need to make it clear to Finley I won't be here in the morning. I saw Kendal's face when she reminded me to tell him and I don't want her to go through that again. It must have been horrible for her. I look into his eyes that are identical to mine and my dads. I need to tell my parents about all this.

"Finley I won't be here when you wake up OK?"

I see his little eyebrows frown.

"Why daddy?"

I take hold of his small hand.

"I don't live here with you and mummy. I'll still see you tomorrow."

"You and mummy need to be boyfriend and girlfriend."

I don't speak straight away. I just look down at him in shock.

"Why do you think that?"

"Logan's mummy and daddy are. I told mummy and she said you're not boyfriend and girlfriend."

Oh I see. I want that too, but I can't tell Finley that.

"Finley, me and mummy haven't seen each other in a long time. We need to be friends again first."

"Then mummy can have another baby?"

I nearly choke. Another baby?

"How about I get to know you a lot better first, before we think about babies."

He thankfully forgets all about me and Kendal and babies when I start to read the book he chose. When I finish, Finley's eyes are closed. I slowly get up from his bed and lightly kiss his forehead.

"Night-night daddy."

I stoke his hair out of his eyes.

"Night Son."

I watch him sleeping for a while; this little boy is changing my life for the better, I can feel it.

I walk downstairs and see that Kendal is in the kitchen standing at the sink. As I walk up to her, I can't help but think I'd love to walk straight behind her and wrap my arms around her waist, kiss her neck and tell her I love her. Instead, I stand beside her and lean back into the corner of the worktop. Kendal looks over to me and smiles.

"Thank you for treating him today. He loved it."

I laugh and look out to the trampoline through the window. When I'd watched Kendal and Finley bouncing, I'd felt like the whole world was right at my feet. Watching those two made me feel so happy, happier than when I'm playing on stage. Leo had elbowed me and told me to get on with them. It was hard work keeping my eyes from Kendal's bouncing tits but I did it. Just about, but I might have looked a few times.

"I loved it too."

I grab a couple of Bulmer's that Max and Leo brought over and we go into the living room. One drink turns into three and I'm happy to see Kendal is a little tipsy. She's always been a bit of a lightweight. She giggles away as I tell her stories from our time away. It's a relief that she finds some of the situations we found ourselves in hilarious.

We're now sitting pretty close and I let my hand glide onto her bare shoulder. She looks up to me and I'm lost in those big blue eyes of hers.

"Jax?"

"Close your eyes."

She does and I softly kiss all of her gorgeous face. Every inch of it. When I stop at her mouth, I see she's smiling.

"That still feels as good as it used too."

I carry on kissing down to her neck and I feel my cock jump to attention when I hear Kendal's soft moan. I fight to not let my hands slip up her loose top and play with those pretty nipples of hers. Instead, I stop kissing her neck and take her mouth. She responds to me and relaxes into the kiss. Her hands grab onto my hair and I can't help but groan. I grab onto her little waist and lift her around so she's straddling me. I see the surprise on her face and she bites that damn lip of hers.

"Jax, should we be doing this?"

"Yes."

I don't let her say anything else and capture her mouth with mine again. I hold her body against me and I feel Kendal's hands across my shoulders and grab my hair again. Kendal starts to grind against me.

"Jax."

She whimpers. I know what she wants. I don't know what I should do. I'm fighting to hold back.

"Please Jax."

Those two words become my undoing. I grab onto the bottom of her top and yank it above her head. I think she's about to protest but Kendal has that naughty smile on her face. I unclip her bra without taking my eyes from hers until Kendal slips her bra away from her arms. I look down to her perfect tits. I've missed these so much and I greedily take the first little bud into my mouth. I look up and see Kendal look up to the ceiling as she moans in bliss. She's still grinding against me. Kendal's hands come from my hair to hold either side of my face. She pulls me away from her luscious nipple with a pop and looks down at me.

"I need more Jax."

"Kendal I don't-"

"Please."

Her voice sounds so dreamy and full of need. I stand with my hands still around Kendal and she giggles. The sound is music to my fucking ears. I let her slide down my body and she takes my hand to lead me up the stairs. I'm a little uncomfortable when we walk by Finley's room. Kendal turns and rolls her eyes at me.

"Honestly Jax, do you think parents stop having sex when they have kids?"

She quietly laughs as she walks into her bedroom and sits on the edge of her bed. I can't have sex with her yet can I?

This is Kendal and I want to take care of her. Not take advantage, but the way she's grinning at me and beckoning with her finger for me to come, it's hard for me to fight my urges. I step into her room and close the door. I stand in front of her and push her down so she's lying with her back on the bed. Her hair fans out over her head. I lean over her with my hands either side of her face.

"I'm not having sex with you."

Her eyes widen.

"I'm not turning you down baby. I am going to make you come. But I won't be putting my dick into your pussy until you tell me that you love me."

I see she takes in a huge breath of air. Her eyes water a little so I give her a kiss. I'm fighting my fucking hardest to hold back, but I need to do this.

"I love you Kendal. Always have, I've never stopped loving you."

We stare at each other for a while and a tear runs down the side of Kendal's face. I wipe it away with my thumb but when I take my hand away she catches hold of me. She doesn't take her eyes away when she kisses my palm. Kendal reaches up and pulls me down on top of her.

~Kendal~

Fucking hell, did Jax just say he loves me?

Sure Sophie told me he does, but it's different when he actually tells me to my face. I'm too scared to say it back and I don't know why. I need him close, so I pull him down closer to me. I need him as close as he can be – but he's already told me he won't put his delicious cock in me. That's what I'm craving for, as soon as I saw him, I craved for him. My body remembers what he can do to me and wants him.

Jax rips my jeans off me and looks between my legs with pure hunger. I know we're moving fast but I've fucking fantasized about this man for four years. I need him and I do love him but I can't make myself say the words yet.

Jax starts by leaning over me and licking my pierced nipple. He plays with my other with his skilled fingers. I think Jax likes my nipple piercing because as he bites and sucks on it he growls and I feel his hardness pressed against my bare thigh.

He kisses down the valley in between my breast and then on the top of my rib cage but then he groans and goes back to my pierced nipple.

"Fucking love this thing."

I feel like laughing at how right I am but I can't because Jax has removed his other hand away from my nipple and onto my wetness. I moan as quietly as I can and my hips rise to meet his touch.

Jax manages to remove his mouth from his favoured nipple and down my stomach.

Jax teases me over my thong with his tongue. He kisses the inside of my legs on either side, teasing me – so when he goes back to my thong – I gasp at the sweet sensation. I can't help myself from grinding against his face. I feel like applauding when Jax strips away the thong and throws it to the floor. His tongue feels like heaven when he glides from bottom to top. I dig my head into the mattress in great pleasure as his mouth destroys me deliciously. It's not long before that talented tongue of his nearly brings me to the edge of pleasure. I haven't had any sex or been touched by a man for so long. This feels so damn good it should be illegal.

"Jax."

I plead. I don't even care that my voice sounds so needy.

"Come Kendal."

I obey his deep husky command and fall apart against his mouth. When I open my eyes I see Jax smiling down at me with the stupid sexy charming smile. Jesus this man is gorgeous. 100% mans man ruggedness, but his face also has that beauty that makes your heart stutter. Well it does to mine anyway.

We face each other on my bed and Jax wraps his arms around me.

"I meant what I said."

"I know."

I feel guilty for not being able to say that I feel the same. I don't know what's keeping me back. Maybe when we have spent more time together I will be able to. This is still all a huge shock to the system. Jax strokes my hair and I feel like I've floated back in time. I feel my eyes getting heavy.

"Babe?"

I open my eyes to see Jax looking down at me again.

"It's getting late."

Oh, he's going. I slowly sit up and follow Jax downstairs. I feel really sad he's going, but its best if he does go. If Finley woke to find Jax in my bed he would think we were together and it would only confuse him. We get to the front door and he strokes my cheek. I really don't want him to go.

"I'm so happy to find you Kendal. You gave me the best present a man could get. You and Finley are my life now. Don't leave me again."

"I won't. I promise."

He gives me a goodbye kiss and cheekily pinches my nipple that leaves me begging for more. By the cheeky smile he flashes before he leaves to go to his car, he knows the effect he has on me. I watch his tight ass as he walks away.

When I get into bed I think about the possibility of maybe giving me and Jax another shot. Not yet though. It's too soon but I'm not going to lie, it's going to be really hard to resist him, he's only just left and my body is craving him, wanting a repeat of what he did tonight, wanting more.

Chapter 7

Two weeks later

These last two weeks have been heaven and hell. Watching Finley get to know Jax has made me unbelievably happy. They're amazing together and that old feeling of guilt creeps up when I watch them because seeing Finley now, makes me realize how much he actually did need Jax.

We haven't had another night like that steamy night two weeks ago. Which is complete torture for me. Jax will sometimes brush against me or he'll run his fingers along the back of my neck. Sometimes he smooths the back of his hand down my arms and places a hand on my knee under the table. When he says goodbye he will let his mouth linger against mine, after an innocent kiss he will whisper sweetness into my ear. He hasn't told me that he loves me again but he has let me know just how much he wants me, which is just as bad to my craving body.

I haven't heard from Harley since that awkward meeting with Jax. I don't know wether I'm glad or not. I've had a good friendship and then relationship with Harley but that situation outside work was just weird.

Today is my day off work and I'm so excited because the girls are all meeting together because Sophie came back from her honeymoon at the weekend. Sophie and Rhys came over the day after they came back because Rhys really wanted to meet Finley. They got on great.

We're meeting at Summer's. Ever since the first time we met there it has become our favourite place to meet and chat.

Today is Tuesday and that means it is Jax's day to take Finley to school, even though I have the day off.

We decided that Tuesdays and Thursdays are Jax's days to do the school run. He has also taken over from my parents when I'm at work and I'm unable to do the school run. My mum was was a little upset at that but I kindly reminded her that she's had four years with Finley where as Jax hasn't, because of me. Jax being the man he is didn't like to upset my parents so offered to arrange it whenever I got my work schedule. I'm happy to say that my parents met Jax and adore him. Well my dad likes him, my mum adores him. There's no awkwardness and it's like he's always been here with us.

This is Finley's last week of school before he finishes for the school summer holidays and that means it's his birthday next week! Finley's last birthdays have left me feeling down because the whole mess with Jax but I'm so excited for his birthday this year. Jax is here now so now all there is to worry about is making sure Finley doesn't eat too much cake. It will be just a happy day. No fake smiles anymore.

Mine and Jax's first little argument since me telling him about Finley was about Finley's birthday party. Finley wants his party at Crazykids, which is a huge indoor play area. It has everything you need, a soft play area complete with tunnels, slides, swings and ball pits. It even has a mini quad racing area. There is a private party area where the party guests can sit and have something to eat and drink and it has a little dance floor area if the kids want a little disco. It's a set price for three hours but Jax wasn't happy with that. He wanted to hire the whole place out and close it for the day so Finley had the whole place to himself. I couldn't allow him to do that, it would cost a fortune.

Jax being Jax wouldn't listen and didn't think twice about paying for Finley to have CrazyKids to himself for the entire day! I'm grateful because Finley will be amazed but I'm a little annoyed he didn't listen to me because it's a little overboard. At the same time I can't stay mad because he looks adorable at how pleased he is. Jax argues his case saying now Finley and his friends can do whatever they want without a time limit which is a bonus.

Jax lets himself in using his own key to the house that he said he needed to have. I didn't argue with him which I think surprised him. I did like the idea of Jax having a key to my house though.

I nearly choke on my cup of tea when I see Jax walk in through the door. He's wearing his dark blue jeans and his tight black shirt that clings to him. The short sleeves letting me see his tattoos down his arms, his messy black hair is hidden under his black flat peek hat. He hasn't shaved so he has the sexy dark shadow along his jaw and chin. What is this man doing to me?

Finley runs straight up to Jax when he hears him enter the house and my heart swells at the sight. After he's fussed over Finley he walks into the kitchen doorway and smiles at me.

"You're looking beautiful today Kendal."

I think I'm blushing and I hear Finley say.

"Mummy is beautiful."

"Yes she definitely is Finley."

I'm Definitely blushing now and I think my cheeks are as red as the jeans that I'm wearing. I don't look anything special today.

"You look good too Jax."

He smiles knowingly at me and I look away so I don't jump

him in front of our son. We talk for the ten minutes he has to spare before he leaves. I walk them to the door and give Finley a kiss goodbye, Jax pauses by the door.

"Are you doing anything today?"

"Meeting the girls in half an hour."

"After?"

I have nothing planned which makes him smile that charming smile.

"You want to go and look around for Finley's birthday together?"

"Sure."

It sounds like a good idea and I agree to text him when I'm leaving the girls.

Maisy is getting out of her car as I pull up in the little car park next to Summer's. We walk in together and find Tanya, Jessica and Sophie all sat at our usual booth. As soon as I've sat my bottom onto the seat Sophie jumps straight in.

"So, how is everything with Jax going?"

She smiles a wicked smile and I grumble.

"Hell."

All the girls frown at me because I haven't told them what happened between me and Jax. If I want to explain I'm going to have to tell them.

"A couple of weeks ago, after Jax had put Finley to bed. We sort of hooked up."

I watch as all of their perfect eyebrows lift. The waitress takes our orders and as soon as she's gone Tanya turns to face me.

"Spill."

I sigh loudly.

"Yeah. Define 'hooking up' to us."

Sophie uses her fingers to quote her words.

"OK. So we had a couple of drinks and Jax started to kiss me which quickly turned into dry humping. My top came off and we moved to my bedroom where we finished."

My words came out in a hushed rush. I don't know why I'm feeling embarrassed telling the girls. I've never had trouble telling them before. Maisy giggles.

"You're going to have to be a little clearer Kendal."

"What did you two do when you went into your room?"

Jessica asks.

"We kissed some more and he went down on me."

I confess.

"So you didn't have sex?"

Tanya asks and I shake my head no.

"He told me he's not going to have sex with me until I confess that I love him."

They all let their mouths hang open before Maisy says.

"He said that?"

"That's so sweet."

Jessica's voice sounds dreamy but Tanya's shaking her head.

"Kendal, that's not hooking up."

Sophie frowns at her.

"Yes it is."

Jessica and Maisy nod in agreement. Tanya just shrugs it off like she doesn't care. Something's up with her. Jessica waits until the waitress leaves after placing our orders on the table.

"Have you told him how you feel?"

Tanya scoffs at her.

"Of course she hasn't, otherwise she wouldn't say she's in hell would she?"

All the girls frown at her this time along with me. Something is definitely eating at Tanya. She's not usually this snappy. Sophie looks at me.

"Why haven't you?"

"I don't know."

"But you do love Jax?"

I nod my yes and Jessica places her hand over mine that's on the table.

"What else did he say?"

"He told me that he loves me."

I leave out all the rest. Jax spoke those words to me so I want to keep them private.

"So why haven't you told him?"

I take my hand out from under hers and hang my head down.

"I don't know Jess."

I really don't know the answer. The girls take pity on me and leave that subject alone for now. Sophie fills us all in on her wonderful honeymoon. It sounds like absolute paradise and it sounds like she spent most of her time there naked.

"Oh Kendal, Finley has got me and Rhys broody for a baby."

I'm shocked. Not because I don't think they should because I think they would be great parents but because she said it out of nowhere.

"Really?"

She nods her head quickly with a huge grin spreading across her face.

"We've decided to not use anything anymore and if it happens, it happens."

We all smile happily for them and congratulate her. Sophie asks me how I feel about being pictured with Jax when we're out.

"It's fine, I guess. It can be annoying sometimes when we're together and when girls ask about Jax while I'm working. I'm OK with it though."

She looks thoughtful and I remember what I had been thinking about at work.

"Soph, what's going to happen with us now? You've been careful to never be seen with Rhys."

"I spoke to Rhys about this last week. I've decided not to hide. I just can't be bothered anymore. You're OK with it and I don't want it to be a strain on mine and Rhys relationship anymore."

I'm glad because I could use her to lean on sometimes and I think she wants the same from me too. Maisy looks back to me.

"Have you thought about Finley?"

"Yeah, me and Jax spoke about it. We're going to be careful to make sure he's safe and not hounded by them. We're not going to hide him away though. If we do then he won't be able to be out with Jax as much and that's not fair either."

We try to question Tanya on her and Leo but we don't get anywhere. She doesn't want to see or hear from him is all she says. None of us are convinced because she used to go on and on about this secret man who was amazing and how no other man ever lived up to him. How could she stop fantasizing about him now? She's not fooling anyone.

At 11:00 I get a text.

JAX: I have a surprise 4 U baby. When will U B free? xxx

I blush a little at his text. I love how he calls me baby.

"Who's that?"

Jessica leans her neck closer to get a peek at my phone but I hold it to my chest so she can't see. Sophie winks at me.

"I'm guessing it's Jax."

I nod.

"He says he has a surprise. I'm meeting with him after you guys. He wants to go shopping for Finley's birthday."

Tanya and Sophie speak at the same time.

"Surprise?"

"Why are you still here?"

I laugh at them and we all finish up. They're all suddenly eager for me to spend time with Jax. There's no more anti-Jax group anymore.

As the girls all get into their own cars Sophie stays beside me.

"So things are OK with you two?"

"Yes they're great Soph. Jax and Finley are amazing together."

"Aw. I'm so happy for you both. Why don't all three of you all come over for dinner tomorrow night?"

"I'm at work tomorrow. What about Friday afternoon? Finley's at my parents on the Saturday."

"Perfect."

Before I drive away I send Jax a text to let him know I'm on my way home.

Chapter 8

~Jax~

I get into my new car and head for Kendal's house. I'd already told Finley I was getting a new car today when I took him to school. He didn't want me to get rid of the shiny fast car, which made me laugh. I assured him the fast car wasn't going but the new car would still be fast. I won't get rid of my Aston Martin anytime soon, I've wanted one for too long. I've bought this new car because after just a few weeks with Finley I need a family friendly car. This is a big surprise for Kendal but small compared to the other surprise I have for her. That won't be ready for another couple of weeks though.

The car I have purchased is a fucking awesome car! It's a Mercedes Benz G class in black. It's got a lot of room, more than the Aston has and a bigger boot which is good for today. I haven't told Kendal but today I'm planning on treating her aswell as Finley. I want to spoil her but I know she won't be happy about it.

After seeing what Kendal's life is like these past two weeks I'm in complete awe of her. She has taken care of our son on her own for four years and she has done a fucking amazing job. She's an un-fucking-believable woman and I want her so bad!

I don't understand why it's taking so long for her to admit her feelings, but she will. I need her to say it. I think back to that night and I wish I could have stayed over and held her all night and woken up in the same house as Finley but that wouldn't have been fair to him. He wouldn't understand. I wonder if Kendal would let me have Finley over for a night.

Two weeks ago I would have thought that was impossible but ever since Sophie and Rhys wedding the guys have changed. The house parties have almost stopped and the couple they have had haven't been their usual style. The music wasn't as loud, it wasn't late and the number of girls had halved. They have been out of the house a lot more though and I'm thinking that maybe they're doing there business elsewhere now. I know if I told them Finley was staying over they would be on their best behaviour. They love Finley so I know they wouldn't mind him staying over. They would stay in with us.

When I pull up outside Kendal's and see her ugly little car parked outside I think of a perfect birthday or Christmas present for her. Kendal would go crazy but once she's mine again she won't be able to complain. I want to take care of Kendal and Finley and if that means buying her a new car then I will.

I let myself in with my own key. I hear the radio on in the kitchen so I head straight there. The back door is open and as I walk past the window by the sink I stop and smile. Kendal is hanging her washing out and wiggling her bottom to the fast dance track that's playing. She doesn't even hear me approach her and gasps when I place my hands on her hips. I would love to grab onto her tight arse. I meant what I said this morning. She looks beautiful everyday.

"Bloody hell Jax. You scared me."

I laugh and step away as I watch her finish hanging out the wet clothes.

"You know, you could help."

"Or I could stay here and watch you."

She blushes and turns away. I remember that hot little body of hers and I want to see it again. The waiting is killing me but it will be worth it. When we step outside Kendal looks puzzled.

"Jax where's your car?"

She looks around at the houses to see if I've parked in front of any other house. Totally missing the huge Mercedes so I outstretch my arm and point to it. I watch as her eyes widen and she gasps.

"You bought a new car?"

"Yep. I thought it would be better for my new family lifestyle."

She surprisingly smiles at me.

"But you love your other car."

I grab hold of her hand and lead her to her seat. When I get in and shut the door behind me I finally respond to her.

"I didn't sell the Aston Kendal."

She stops flicking through her mobile and snaps her head in my direction.

"Are you serious?"

I nod and start driving away.

"Jax that is ridiculous and a lot of money!"

"Kendal you don't have to worry about my money. OK?"

"Yeah well excuse me if I don't want you to waste your hard earned money."

I laugh a little at that. She's so fucking cute.

"Kendal there's no chance of that happening. Don't worry about it."

She finally lets it go and huffs as she sits back in her seat. She looks back at her phone and frowns.

"What's the matter?"

She shakes her head and bites her lip.

"Kendal?"

She exhales loudly.

"Fine. I'm looking though websites and all they have is pictures of us. They seem to think I'm the one for you. Why do they think that?"

I guess I should have told her about this before we left. So I explain to her about everything that me and Angie had arranged.

"So that is why they think I'm this special girl? Because we're on and off all the time? Gee I guess I look like a dumb bitch."

I frown at her road.

"Why would you think that?"

"Hmm, let me think. Maybe because all these years you have been shagging your way through so many girls while we're supposed to have been on and off. I just look like I'm a dumb girlfriend to a rich guy."

I didn't think about it looking that way but she's not right. She doesn't fucking get it.

"You can't care what the media prints Kendal. Your friends and family are the only ones that matter."

"Yeah well I care."

The rest of the drive is quiet. I need to meet John and Paul before we go shopping. They're the bands bodyguards and I hate using them but I want to keep Kendal safe. Because she's in one of her little stubborn moods she doesn't even kick up a fuss when I introduce her to the huge men in suits. She politely says hello and turns back in her seat, I don't miss the glance John and Paul share. Probably thinking Kendal's different to all the other girls they've been around from the band. Thank fuck for that.

Chapter 9

We pull up behind Harrods at the private entrance. I prepare myself and wait for when Kendal figures out where we are.

"Why are we here Jax?"

I ignore her and get out the car. When I open her door and hold her hand as she gets out I answer.

"Before we shop for Finley, I want to treat you."

She takes her hand out of mine and crosses them over her chest.

"No way Jax. You're not spending your money on me."

I see John and Paul both look shocked at Kendal for saying this. They thought she would be some gold digging woman, Kendal's nothing like that.

"Look, I don't care what you say. I am treating you today Kendal."

I wrap my arm around her back and guide her to the entrance of the shop. Kendal tries to hold her body to the spot.

"Fine. You stay here and I will go and get a personal shopper to spend as much as I want on you."

She eyes me and I see her cracking. She doesn't like that

idea at all. So I taunt her some more.

"No limits."

Her arms open and she huffs loudly as she storms to where John and Paul are waiting at the entrance.

"I cannot believe you Jax Parker."

I hold back my laugh because I don't want to piss her off even more. I want her to enjoy today.

Inside Harrods it isn't so bad. Nobody approaches us but that's probably because some of these women probably don't know who I am and the fact we have two huge bodyguards standing beside us scares them off.

Kendal gives everything a quick glance but not for too long. Probably thinking that if I see her looking at something for longer than a minute I will buy it for her. To my relief, a saleswoman approaches us asking if we need any help.

"Yes actually. I want to spoil my girl here. You think you could help?"

I see the woman's eyes sparkle and I ignore Kendal's glare from beside me.

"Follow me."

The saleswoman takes us to a private room with two sofas and two changing rooms. As Kendal talks to the woman I tell John and Paul they can wonder for a bit while we're in here. I see the saleswoman leave in a hurry, eager to spend my money. As soon as she is gone, Kendal lets me have it.

"I can't believe you. You said if I came you wouldn't do this."

"But you weren't shopping."

"Yes I was, I just didn't see anything that I liked."

"Liar."

She stares at me for a while and then laughs. She sits down next to me on the little sofa and huffs.

"You're still so stubborn Jax."

I scoff.

"Me? You need to look at yourself woman."

We happily chat until only fifteen minutes later the saleswoman returns with two other girls. They are each rolling in a clothes rack full of clothes. I see Kendal's eyes widen and she whispers.

"Oh my God."

~Kendal~

When the pushy saleswoman comes back she has two young girls with her. They are all pushing along a clothes rack full of clothes. How many clothes do they think Jax is going to buy me? I really don't want Jax to buy me anything, especially from here! Jax shouldn't be buying me clothes but I know how much of a stubborn man he can be. No matter how much I don't want him to, I know I won't be able to change his mind.

To my dismay the saleswoman, who we now know as Janet, has stayed with Jax and me while I try the clothes on.

The first outfit she gives me is gorgeous. This is totally me. Skinny purple jeans, simple white top with a black leather jacket. I hesitate to try it on though. I know these clothes aren't going to be cheap. I look to Jax, he's sitting, leaning back on one of the sofa's with his right foot over his left knee.

"Jax, why don't we go somewhere else?"

Maybe somewhere cheaper? Jax's smile drops and he comes to stand in front of me.

"Kendal."

Jax places his hand softly on my cheek and strokes his thumb along my cheekbone.

"I want to treat you, no arguments."

I open my mouth to argue but see Jax's face harden, so I don't answer and walk into the changing room where Janet has already hung up some outfits.

I decide to try the outfit that I like the most on first, which is the one Janet showed me before I started to complain to Jax. I slip on the purple jeans which feel incredibly soft and then reach for the white top. Oh shit. I was wrong. This isn't a simple white top. Janet had tucked it into the leather jacket backwards so I didn't see the front. On the front of the white top is a big Chanel sign. It's a fucking Chanel top! I close my eyes as I put it over my head because I don't want to see how much it is. I look in the mirror when I put on the leather jacket and my eyes widen. I look fucking hot! Like a hot rocker chick. I love this outfit but I don't want Jax to buy it for me.

"Come on Kendal."

I don't wait any longer. I take in a calming breath and open the door to the changing room and walk out into the mirrored room. I notice how Jax's eyes widen a little when I come out. As soon as I see that little reaction from him I hide my smile.

I make a choice to enjoy this and make Jax suffer in return. Suddenly trying on these clothes doesn't seem so bad now and I spin around at Janet's praise before I try on my next outfit.

An hour later I'm trying on the last item of clothing. I haven't told Jax but I have had some favorites out of all the clothes I've tried on. Every time I come out Janet says yes or no and when I hand it out before trying something else she puts them onto the yes or no hanger. The yes section is looking pretty big and I cringe when I see it but I notice that all my favorites are in it.

Now I have on a black fitting dress that I know Jax is going to love. Jax sure has suffered through my dress up game. With every outfit I have tried on his eyes got heavier with lust. I enjoyed it very much and I'm going to enjoy watching his reaction to this dress. I really like this dress and I don't care if Janet says yes or no, I want this dress. It's black and fitting, my curves look smooth and sexy. Most of the dress is in see-through lace, apart from the sections that cover my private areas. There's a black material panel that goes across my breasts so it hides them well but you can still see the swell of my breasts at the top. To hide my bottom area, is another black panel. This one goes diagonal from the curve above my hip on my left, down across my belly button to where my underwear is on my right side. On my thighs the panel goes across diagonally again from left to right. It shows a lot of thigh on my left leg through the lace and I smile at my reflection.

When I walk out the changing room I look straight at Jax and don't take my eyes away from him. He sits up straight when I walk out and I can see him clenching him jaw and his eyes devour me. I do a slow turn and see in the reflection of the mirror that Jax's eyes widen when they see how my bottom is sculpted by the dress. When I turn back Jax is standing, staring at me with hunger. I don't even notice Janet and don't look in her direction as Jax speaks to her in a low husky tone.

"Janet I think we need shoes."

"Erm, yes OK Mr. Parker."

With Janet gone, Jax stalks me. When he reaches me he places a hand between my collar bones to push me back against the mirrored wall.

"Fucking hell Kendal you're killing me."

"Why?"

He licks his lips and looks back to my face. I know exactly why.

"I wanna bury my cock in you right now baby. You look so fucking sexy in that dress."

I act like I'm not bothered by his words but really they're setting me on fire as he tells me exactly what he wants to do to my body.

When Janet comes back in with another girl, each holding four shoe boxes, Jax doesn't even move away from me. Janet acts like there's nothing going on but the younger girl is blushing. Before Jax moves away he whispers in my ear.

"I'm fucking buying you this dress."

He adjusts himself before he goes to sit back down. When I get changed back into my own clothes I can't help but smile. That felt good.

Jax sets aside a pair of Valentino stud strap biker boots and a pair of Kurt Geiger open toe shoe boots.

Janet and the young girl take away the clothes and shoes

that have been chosen for me. Jax and I walk behind them and I walk around a little bit as Jax pays because now I feel bad for enjoying myself and making him think I want him to buy me the clothes. Of course I love them but I hate the fact Jax is spending his money on me. I won't lie, it does make me feel special but at the same time I feel guilty. Two men walk us out with our bags and put them in the back of the car before we leave with John and Paul.

"You know Finley would have loved that."

I laugh.

"Yeah he would."

When we arrive at the toy store there's a few paparazzi waiting for us. Jax takes hold of my hand as we walk out of the car. As we walk hand-in-hand in between John and Paul some of the paparazzi shout questions.

"Are you together?"

"Why have you been hiding Kendal?"

"Is it true you're getting married?"

What? Married? Where do they get this stuff?

Then, one of the first things that I see when we walk in I have to buy.

"Jax, look at this!"

I pull Jax along to the display. It's a play mat in the style of a drum kit. You get two drum sticks and just hit the drums and symbols. Jax has a go on the one open for display, tapping away at the drums.

"This is fucking awesome."

He picks up a box and we find the section for the Nintendo DS. I grab him a red one and Jax takes is off me.

"No Jax, I'm buying him this."

"I will."

I glare at him. No way is he buying Finley everything. He's paid for his party, my clothes and I want to buy this.

"No Jax. I haven't bought him anything yet."

"Fine, but I'm buying the games."

He goes to grab a basket and fills it with games. We have a stroll around the rest of the store and in the back there are battery powered cars. I see Jax smile and he quickly walks over to them. He keeps on walking until he stops at the black Range Rover at the end. Oh my God that is fucking adorable! I look at the price and shake my head.

"Yes Kendal."

"Jax, it's too much."

He takes a card beside the car.

"Nothing is too much for my little boy."

This statement from Jax completely stops me from complaining. What can I say to that?

Jax gets the car delivered to his house and we pay for the rest. When we step outside the paparazzi are still there.

"Why are you in a toy store?"

"Are you pregnant?"

"How do you feel about Jax being a playboy?"

I ignore their stupid questions and get into the car.

Chapter 10

The rest of the week goes by in a mad blur. While Finley was at school on the Wednesday Jax came by and we spoke about every media wise. He explained everything his managing team told the press about me and the whole story about us being forever in love. It's a romantic story and I really wished it were true. I'm really grateful that Jax thought to spin off a whole story about the three of us to protect Finley from being shunned. I'm a little worried how Finley will be when he's out with Jax and paparazzi are there.

Jax took Finley out that Wednesday night for pizza with Rhys, Max and Leo. Jax said he loved spending time with the guys, which I knew he would. Apparently some paparazzi were there to get their first pictures of Finley. Jax told me how Finley just held onto his hand and smiled at the cameras which I'm very pleased about.

The day after Finley went to dinner with his dad, the pictures were on the internet and there was one in the newspaper with the headline.

Jax's Secret Son Comes Out Of Hiding

All the articles are positive and like our story. They have all bought the lie about Jax's decision to keep me and Finley a secret. The internet articles think Finley is adorable and a little version of Jax, which they love.

On Thursday the paper ran a story on Sophie and me, loving that two of Decoys women have come out of hiding. The main picture was of me and Sophie standing outside of Summers when we were talking the other day. It worried me that I didn't even know anyone was there and that they can take a picture of you without you even knowing. Good thing Sophie already decided she wasn't hiding anymore.

Maisy has actually found a website dedicated to Decoy, Sophie and me. Calling me and Sophie the Degirls, which I thought was pretty clever and hilarious. It's cute how they have designed the page, Sophie and Rhys and then Me and Jax. There are pictures of us all and people commenting how much they like us or sometimes disliking us. Hating because they think me and Sophie are taking Rhys and Jax away from them. They have a section on mine and Sophie's friends which are obviously the girls and Max and Leo have their own section. There are girls on this website planning out how to get their own attention by becoming the next Degirl. It's all very funny and unreal.

Finley, bless him, has his own little section. Pictures from that last two days are up there. The girls love that he looks just like Jax. Somebody has dedicated a website to just me and Sophie called the Degirls. Pictures taken by the paparazzi are on there too. Girls talk about mine and Sophie's fashion. I didn't even realize I had a fashion sense. I just get up and throw whatever it is that I want to wear for that day. But girls on here think I have blog worthy fashion taste. It's embarrassing but yet flattering at the same time. It's a good job Jax bought me those gorgeous clothes when he did, even though I still can't believe I let him buy them me. It's all fucking unreal. Since reuniting with Jax my life has dramatically changed.

I get back into my car from taking Finley to school when my phone alerts me that I have a text message.

TANYA: Girls! I need a night out in the clubs! Please tell me UR free 4 tomorrow night!

She's not in work today so I text her back before I drive off. I tell her I'm up for a good night out. Finley's at my parents' tomorrow night anyway. Fingers crossed all of the girls can come.

As I drive off I can help but think about Tanya. I hope she's OK, I'm a little worried about her and that message seemed a little desperate of her.

At work she's fine until I mention Jax. Anything related to Leo shuts her off. Since the wedding she's not acting herself at all. From what I've seen and heard about Leo, he's not exactly the same either. What is up with those two? Why could it be so bad between them and why is everyone just finding out about it now?

I don't finish work until 5:00, so Jax collects him from school and takes him back to my house so he can be ready for dinner at Rhys and Sophie's when I finish work.

When I get home I quickly change out of my work clothes in a daze. I've been stressing myself about Tanya all day. I've text her to ask what's bothering her but all she says is it's nothing. I'm not buying it and when I'm ready we leave in Jax's big car. I think Jax said it was a Mercedes. I like it a lot better than his Aston Martin.

When we pull up outside Rhys and Sophie's beautiful home Finley is way too excited. Before we get out the car Jax turns to look at me.

"Are you OK babe?"

"Yeah."

He gives me that look that tells me he isn't buying it.

"Alright. I'm worried about Tanya. She wants to go out tomorrow night but I'm just worried about her. She's not herself."

Jax frowns.

"Yeah I know what you mean. Leo's the same."

He places his hand on top of mine and gives it a reassuring squeeze.

"They will sort it out. Stop worrying."

"Mummy! Daddy! I wanna get out now!"

We both smile and turn to look at Finley in the back. He's trying to get out of his seatbelt and frowning at us. As soon as Jax lets Finley out he goes running straight into Rhys outstretched arms shouting "Uncle Rhys".

~~*

Three hours later, Jax is driving me and Finley home after a huge dinner that Sophie cooked. There was way too much food. Not that the guys and Finley were bothered, they tried their best to eat every last bite. It's really quiet in the car because as soon as Jax started to drive Finley fell asleep.

"So you looking forward to your girls night?"

I knew that was bothering him, I saw his body slightly tense when Sophie told Rhys about Tanya's text. At dinner Rhys and Jax had both taken an interest in our night out. They told us we were to take John and Paul. I wasn't having that.

"No way. It's supposed to be a girls night."

Jax gave me a stern look.

"Kendal you and Sophie have been getting attention lately. We want you to be safe so you will be taking them with you."

Sophie groaned.

"This isn't going to be much of a girls night and I doubt the girls will be impressed."

Rhys smiled at Sophie, unlike the intense look I was getting from Jax.

"They will be in the background. You won't even notice them."

I hold back my scoff. John and Paul are huge, bulky men. There's no way they can blend into the background but they get their own way and the men in suits have to babysit us.

Now I turn to look at Jax driving. I don't know why he's so bothered about me going out. I'm not stupid and I have been out before. Does he expect me to stay in all the time? Definitely not. Finley is at my parents tomorrow night, so I want a night out with my girls and that's what I am going to do.

"Yep. Tanya says she needs it and I'm looking forward to it."

He slowly nods his head.

"Rhys rang up the club called Blitz. You're in the V.I.P area for the night."

"V.I.P?"

Why has he put us in V.I.P? Maybe Rhys rang up the club but I bet it was Jax who suggested it.

"It will be safer."

This makes me so mad. He is stomping all over girls night!

"Jax this is ridiculous. We're taking the men in black, isn't that enough?"

He frowns out the window, not taking his eyes off the road.

"I won't risk your safety Kendal. People will be drinking and some people can get a bit too friendly when you're a familiar face. You will all have unlimited drinks and your own private dance floor. You will still have your girls night, just now Rhys and I won't be worrying back home about you."

Apart from the entire safety lecture, the unlimited drinks and our own dance floor did sound great. Plus Blitz is the best club in town, I can't really argue.

"Well I'll have to run it by Tan because it was her night."

I see the corner of his mouth lift. The smug bastard.

When we get to my house Jax takes Finley inside and helps me get him ready for bed. We make our way downstairs and have a quiet drink together in the living room. On the same sofa as last time.

"Do you think that I could maybe have Finley over for the night?"

I'm shocked by his question but I don't disagree with him. I know Finley would love that.

"It doesn't matter. We can wait until I have my own place or just until Finley knows me better."

I stop his rambling.

"Jax, that wouldn't be a problem. Finley would love to."

"Really?"

I laugh at his happy face.

"You look like Finley."

This makes him smile even wider.

"You don't mind?"

"Of course I don't. As long as Max and Leo behave and don't have girls over when Finley's there then it's OK by me. Finley knows and loves you enough. He's off school for six weeks now so you can have him over whenever you want."

Before I know it Jax's lips are on mine, I take it that he's happy. Soon the kiss turns passionate but he won't take it any further than kissing no matter what I do or how much I beg, and I do shamelessly beg him. But he won't budge and I go to bed alone and very unsatisfied again. If this torture carries on much longer I'm going to take a leaf out of Tanya's book and buy myself a fucking vibrator.

Chapter 11

The next morning Finley wakes me up by bouncing on my bed as usual. I know that it's early but before I can check the time I hear my phone vibrate on the table beside my bed. Before I answer I see that it's Tanya calling.

"Hello?"

My voice is croaky from sleep.

"Sophie told me what Rhys and Jax have organised for tonight."

I'm relived to hear that she doesn't sound pissed.

"Yeah, they're over reacting."

"They're right though you know. After all, you two are Degirl's now!"

I can hear the bitch laughing.

"Jax also mentioned unlimited drinks."

"Really? Well that's fucking awesome! A free night at the hottest club in town. Tonight is gonna be amazing!"

I'm shocked. I thought she wouldn't like this at all. After all the two people have organized this are Leo's best friends. I suppose when you throw in V.I.P and unlimited drinks she overcomes her hatred for the man.

"What time are we meeting?"

I hear her now groaning down the phone.

"I'm at work until six. Let's got ready at your house. I can *be there for seven and I'll bring drinks."*

"Great. See you then."

When I hang up I'm surprised that Finley doesn't demand his breakfast. He has been watching me while I was talking to Tanya and he's still looking straight at me.

"Can I talk to daddy?"

"It's early honey. He might still be sleeping."

"It's OK mummy."

I look down at my phone and see it's 8:00am.

"Please mummy?"

Oh what the hell. I'm sure he won't mind and anyway, he needs to get experience for all things parents do. I find Jax's number and hand my phone over to Finley.

"Make sure you say sorry for waking him up."

He nods at me with the cutest look on his face. I know the moment that Jax answers because his little face lights up.

"Morning daddy! It's me! Were you sleeping?"

He waits for his answer and then laughs.

"You're lazy daddy."

I smile as I get out of bed and get ready as I listen to Finley's side of the conversation. When I'm dressed and looking presentable I decide it's time for Finley to say goodbye to Jax.

"Come on then rock star, say bye to daddy. It's time for

breakfast."

"Ohh. Bye daddy, I have breakfast now."

I sit on the bed by Finley and wait.

"Yes mummy going to do my juice, biscuits and toast.........OK daddy.....love you.....Bye."

Aw he's so cute. When we get downstairs I make Finley what he wants for breakfast. When I put his toast on the table in front of him he smiles up at me.

"Thank you mummy. You're the best."

"Aw thank you Finley."

I kiss his forehead.

"Daddy told me to say it."

Good enough.

An hour later we decide to walk down to the park. We're not there for long when I get a text from Jax.

JAX: Loved Fin's wakeup call. What R U 2 up 2? x

ME: I'm glad U liked it. Sorry it was early, I couldn't tell him no. We R at the park :) x

JAX: I'll B there in 15 x

I had a feeling he would say that and I feel a little guilty for not asking him myself but it was early. I thought he would roll over and go back to sleep. I think I would have if I had the choice. I decide not to tell Finley and let him be surprised. So me and Finley play while we wait for Jax.

I see a car stop near the park and I see Jax get out and run towards us. It's not until the car drives away that I notice Max driving it, waving to me. I try my best not to visibly drool at the sight of Jax. Nobody should be able to look that good.

~Jax~

As soon as I got the text back from Kendal to let me know they were at the park, I had to go. Max was already up and offered me a lift in his car.

When the park was in sight I could see Kendal chasing after Finley. I could tell they both had smiles on their faces. They looked so happy and I couldn't wait to join them.

I didn't miss the way Kendal looked at me as I approached them. She looked good enough for me to eat. Absolutely gorgeous.

As soon as Finley saw me he ran straight up to me. That's when the games began, we were on our own in this part of the park so we could be as silly as we wanted to be. You could have heard Finley laughing a mile away when he was on my shoulders as we chased after Kendal. At one point, I couldn't fight the urge to not touch Kendal any longer. I ran up to her when she was least expecting it, which made her squeal in surprise. I swung her around to face me in my arms until I had her positioned so she had her legs around my waist and her head was looking up to sky as she laughed. When she looked down at me her laughing stopped but she was still smiling. I spun around in a circle which made her laugh again, begging me to stop. I could see Finley laughing at us. This is what I want everyday.

After we have had enough of playing we decide to go back to Kendal's for something to eat. As we're walking back hand in hand, Finley in the middle. I notice there is a few paparazzi around. I don't think Kendal has noticed them because she's happily smiling.

I've kept quiet about Kendal going out tonight because I'm jealous. Other men will see her tonight, not me. I know it's stupid but that's the truth. She isn't mine yet and men will look because she is stunning. I want them to know she's off limits. Leo wants to turn up uninvited, I don't want to spy but I'm not going to lie, it is tempting. I've told John and Paul to keep a close eye on them all and if anyone attempts anything they're to ring me. Leo's all for it, so is Rhys to a certain extent but Max disagrees. I don't question Leo's reason because I know without asking his reason is because he wants to see Tanya.

We manage to make it to Kendal's with no interference from the paparazzi but I know they're snapping away. Greedy to get a picture of the new celebrity rock family. This is why I want Kendal safe for tomorrow, she doesn't realize how much her day to day life is going to change.

We're sat around the kitchen table eating our sandwiches when I decide to send Kendal a text, even though she's only sitting opposite me.

ME: Can I ask Fin about staying at mine? x

She looks up from her phone and nods at me. I look at Finley who has a mouth full of food.

"Finley, if you're good for mummy. Would you like to sleep at my house?"

He breaks into a huge smile and quickly swallows. Which gets me a little worried because it seems to take him a while because there's so much food in his mouth.

"Today?"

"No not today pal. You have to be good first."

Finley's smile drops and I feel like shit. Kendal thankfully helps me out.

"You're going to mama and granddads tonight Finley."

"I wanna go daddy's."

He crosses his arms across his chest and I try my fucking hardest not to smile.

Chapter 12

~Kendal~

Jax leaves a little after my mum comes to collect Finley at 5:00 so he can say bye. I jump in the shower so I don't have to have one once the girls are here.

Tanya turns up right on time at 7:00 shortly followed by Sophie, Jessica and Maisy. When everyone's here Tanya sets down five glasses and fills them with her choice of alcohol.

"Right girls. Tonight we are getting totally wasted."

We all exchange a worried glance.

"Oh come on! Look how much has changed in the past two months. We all need a good night out."

I notice that she keeps glancing over at me when she's making that little speech of hers. I decide that I do need a crazy night out so I walk up to one of the drinks and take a big gulp and then wish that I hadn't.

"Christ that's fucking strong Tan!"

Tanya takes a drink from her glass and smiles.

"Perfect."

John and Paul are going to pick us up at 10:00pm so we spend the time drinking the alcohol Tanya brought over and slowly getting ready. By the time we're all ready we're beyond tipsy.

We have our dark clubbing make-up on and sexy little dresses. I have decided to wear the lacy black dress that Jax bought for me. It will probably drive him crazy but he's stomping all over our girls night so I feel I'm getting even with him if I wear the sexy dress. Even though Rhys and Jax did get us into V.I.P in the hottest club in town, they still took charge. Tanya soon demanded that there was to be no man talk tonight. I think she just wanted to make sure nobody mentioned Leo while we were out.

I can't say I'm surprised that when John and Paul knock on I see they have a limo waiting for us. Tanya and Jessica make happy whooping noises while they make their way into the limo. When it's just me and Sophie we share a knowing look. Our men are so stubborn. Oh shit wait, Jax isn't mine. Well I hope he will be but we aren't together. I need to stop thinking about Jax so when Maisy hands me a glass of champagne I eagerly drink.

When we stop in front of the loud club there's a long line of people waiting to get inside. John and Paul help us all out and I'm surprised when I see a few flashes. I look up to see there's a few paparazzi standing to the side of the club taking photos of us. They're probably here because seeing as this is one of the top clubs, seeing a celebrity is most likely.

I'm dumbfound when they start shouting mine and Sophie's names. I'm thankful to have John and Paul with us as they guide us into the thriving club. Just before we step into the doors I catch sight of Harley near the front of the que of people. I'm slightly worried to see him because our last encounter wasn't so good but when he waves and smiles at me it eases my worries. I'm sure that whole scene was because he was jealous of Jax. He's just the same old Harley.

When we step inside the building the loud music immediately vibrates my body.

We take advantage of the free drinks that we were promised and have a great time. I'm surprised that Jax was right about John and Paul, I hardly notice them. In fact I keep forgetting they're here with us.

A couple of hours later at midnight me, Tanya and Maisy really want to join the big crowd of people on the dance floor. John and Paul don't really like that idea so I'm begging John while Tanya tries to work her magic on Paul.

"Come on John, please?"

"You guys will have a view from up here to watch us."

She strokes Pauls suit jacket and I notice Paul freeze in place.

"Alright fine but you stay on that dance floor and no more drinks until you're back up here."

We agree and down we go, laughing on the way to the clubs main dance floor. As we make our way into the middle of the crowd, I notice that we get a few curious looks.

We have a great time dancing our 'single dance' as Jessica calls it. As I'm swaying against Maisy I glance up to the V.I.P area and wave up to Sophie and Jessica who are dancing near the glass banister wall. They both wave back but I can see Jessica has her phone in her hand. Probably texting lover boy Sam. All the drinks I have drank are catching up with my system and I am feeling so drunk right now. We form a small circle and sing loudly to each other.

During a fast song that I love I feel two large hands hold onto my waist and a body press against my back. I turn around with an angry look on my face and demand they let go however, when I face the man I see it's Harley I relax and smile up at him. Letting Harley sway me to the music. He leans down and speaks directly into my ear.

"Hey beautiful."

Just as I'm about to answer him I feel somebody else press against my back again. Who is it now? Harley is still holding me so I turn my head around and gasp.

"Jax!"

~Jax~

I'm sat at Rhys house with the guys, when at 9:00pm I get a text from Jessica. When I open it I choke on my beer. Max smacks my back laughing.

"What's the fucking matter with you?"

He leans over my shoulder and looks down at my phone. Before I can think to hide the picture Max has already seen it.

"You lucky bastard."

I shove him away.

"Forget you saw that."

"Not likely."

Rhys approaches to take my phone away but I hold it to my chest but I don't see Leo reach from behind me and take it. Max holds me back while Rhys and Leo both look at my phone with raised eyebrows. Rhys hands me back my phone.

"Ask Jess if she has one of Soph."

I laugh as I send Jessica a text back. I look back to the picture she sent me of Kendal. She's wearing the sinful black lace dress. Playfully posing sexually, she probably has no idea that her best friend sent this.

Rhys gets a text a couple of minutes later and I know that Jessica sent him by the looks of his satisfied smirk. Leo goes to look at his phone but Rhys puts his phone away.

"You little fuckers aren't looking at my wife."

Leo sits back down like a grumpy teenager.

"I say we just go."

Max sits on the arm of the chair Leo is sat in and punches his arm.

"Leave her man."

"Shut up."

No guessing who they're talking about. My phone vibrates again.

JESSICA: *Here's a little gift 4 Leo*

I scroll down and see that it's a picture of Tanya in the same pose as Kendal. I can't help but laugh to myself, Rhys being the closest to me looks down at my phone and laughs with me.

"I think you should send that to Leo."

Leo looks up and frowns. I look to Max.

"Come here Max. Do you think I should?"

Max quickly walks over and his eyes widen at the picture I show him.

"Fucking hell. The way he pines over her he'll come in his trousers."

Leo now walks up to us.

"What are you talking about?"

I forward the message to him.

"Look at your phone."

When he does we laugh at the look on his face.

"I wanna go to that club."

"Will you just let the girls have a good night? Leave them."

Max has no idea what it's like to feel like this over a girl. I'm shocked that Leo does.

"If you care about the girls as much as you say you do. Are you happy them going out drunk like this."

"Especially now Kendal and Sophie get attention."

Rhys adds and I see it gets to Max as he shifts where he stands.

"Unless John and Paul get in touch just leave them alone. They will be fine in V.I.P anyway."

We try our best to forget about our women. We go into the studio Rhys has built in his house to try out a few new songs to take our minds of them and it does work.

That is until I get from John informing me three of the girls begged him to go down to the main dance floor and he's watching them. I can guess who those three girls are. I get a text from my little inside spy, Jessica, straight after John's.

JESSICA: Kendal, Tan and Maisy down on the dance floor. Just 2 let U no Harley is here 2

I immediately stand and get ready to leave. Leo is straight away at my side.

"What's up?"

"Girls went down to the dance floor and that fucker Harley is there."

Max begins to walk with us, Rhys is already following. He doesn't like the sound of Harley ever since I told him about out little run in before. Rhys laughs as he locks up his house and gets into my Aston Martin.

All thoughts of Harley getting near my girl making me drive faster towards the club. I park around the back where they're a couple of limos waiting for their V.I.P's.

As soon as we enter we're taken straight into V.I.P. I see Sophie and Jessica dancing and laughing away. Sophie drunkenly wraps herself around Rhys when she sees him. I walk straight over to John who's standing by the glass banister which looks down to the crowd of dancers.

I spot the girls and smile as I watch them dance. They sing the lyrics to each other and keep on hugging. Something I've noticed drunk girls do a lot. The girls dance together, swaying against each other to the song. Max and Jessica wonder over to me.

"That is so hot."

"That is called the single dance."

She giggles but I tense. Kendal shouldn't be taking part in a single dance. I watch Kendal as she moves her perfect little body. I feel a little guilty for showing up but I can't help but want to dance with her. To feel her grinding over my body.

My thoughts stop when I see Harley on the edge of the dance floor. He's looking right at me. He smirks as he walks into the crowd of dancers. Leo stands close.

"Why is that dude smiling at you?"

"That's him."

I watch him making his way through the crowd and as he gets closer to Kendal he gives me a smile. He knows where she is. I don't want him anywhere near her. I walk towards the stairway that leads to the main area of the club. Rhys grabs onto my arm.

"What are you doing?"

"That fucker is going to Kendal."

"You're going to get recognised down there."

"I don't give a fuck. You stay here with Sophie and Jessica."

When I'm out the V.I.P area I make my way towards Kendal. I don't even notice that Leo and Max have come with me until I hear Max curse when we see Kendal in Harley's arms.

He smiles right at me over Kendal's shoulder and fucking winks at me! I walk right up to them and don't even answer Kendal when she shouts my name. I'm too angry looking at the bastard who's still smiling at me.

"Well, well, well. If it isn't the rock star."

"Get your fucking hands off her."

He turns Kendal's head so she faces him again.

"I'm dancing with my girl here. If you don't mind."

Like fuck is Kendal his girl.

"She isn't your girl."

"And she isn't yours."

"What's going on?"

Tanya walks into our little circle glaring at us all. I notice she doesn't look Leo's way. Kendal finally steps out of Harleys grasp.

"That's what I'd like to know."

Max steps closer to Kendal, Tanya and Maisy.

"I think you girls should go back to V.I.P."

This makes Harley laugh. He looks directly at Kendal.

"Thought you wasn't interested in the money Kendal. Is that what I have to do? Flash the cash and you spread your legs."

Kendal gasps and I lunge forward, Max and Leo close.

"Don't you fucking dare talk to her like that!"

"And what are you gonna do?"

I stare him down. Harley gets a £20 note out his pocket and hands it out to Kendal who frowns at him.

"Here darling. Can I have a dance now?"

I don't even think about it. I give him a hard punch which slams him down to the floor. John and Paul immediately appear and lead us all out the club the way we came in. Good, I want to finish the fucking prick.

Chapter 13

~Kendal~

We are all taken outside, in to what appears to be a dirty old car park, I notice a couple of limos and Jax's car. Max holds onto both mine and Maisy's hands.

Jax and Harley are stood face to face shouting insults at one another.

From the look on Jax's face; it's obvious that he's going to lose his temper at any minute.

I was shocked when Jax hit Harley! He hit him so hard, that he fell to the floor! But what astounded me even more was when I heard the vile, vicious words that Harley had said about me. Harley isn't the nice guy that he used to be.

Max tucks me under his arm and kisses my temple. I know he's reassuring me, letting me know it's going to be OK and I appreciate the gesture.

Tanya is standing on my other side with Leo right beside her. Rhys has just stepped out with Sophie and Jessica; they all run straight over to us.

I'm relieved to see that John and Paul are standing close to Jax. I don't want him to have a fight.

As soon as Harley moves to attack Jax, John quickly tackles him to the floor.

"No John! Leave him to me!"

John doesn't seem happy but he nods at Jax. Max keeps a

tight grip on me as Jax and Harley fight. Rhys leans in close.

"Don't watch."

I wish I could turn away but I can't.

I have to be sure that Jax is OK and if I look away, I'd still be able to hear them. I don't understand why nobody is stopping the fight, but Max says he has to do this.

Harley gets punched down to the floor again, only this time he stays down. He's breathing heavily and looking up to the night sky. I run straight into Jax's arms and he squeezes me tight.

"You stupid man."

"I had to fight for the girl I love."

I snuggle closer into his body.

"I love you too."

Jax immediately grips my shoulders and pulls me back to look at me. His eyes are wide in shock, he then kisses me hard.

When Jax finally let's go of me, he instructs John and Paul to take care of Harley. He holds my hand as he walks me to his car. It's a good job we arrived in the limo, because Jax doesn't seem to care how everybody else is going to get home.

When he sits beside me it's quiet for a couple of minutes and I can't help but wonder if Jax is angry with me.

"I'm sorry you had to see that Kendal. I couldn't let him talk to you like that."

"It wasn't nice. I thought you were angry with me."

Jax frowns in confusion.

"Why?

I shrug my shoulders.

"Baby I'm not angry at you. Are you OK?"

I nod and when we pull up in front of my house Jax sweetly kisses my lips. When he pulls away he has a cheeky grin on his face.

"You said you loved me."

"Yes I did."

His face is close enough to kiss. So I do, right on his nose. His hands glide over my dress.

"I can't believe you wore this dress."

I can't help but laugh. I look at his beautiful face; He's perfect. You would think his piercings would put me off but they don't. Jax lifts one of his hands and rubs his finger over one of my nipples. The one that I have pierced which makes me gasp. He kisses me, with pure male hunger and desire. I remember what has happened. I've told Jax that I love him and that means he will finally have sex with me. I deepen the kiss.

"God that tongue bar drives me crazy."

"Want me to put it somewhere else?"

That seems to end our kissing.

"Kendal you've been drinking."

"But you said-"

"I know what I said, but I want you completely sober when we have sex."

"But I'm not that drunk."

That's a lie.

"And I want you to be mine."

I try to catch my breath before I speak.

"What?"

Jax's face turns serious; he places his hand over my cheek.

"Kendal I want you to be mine."

"Yours?"

"Mine."

His voice sounds like a growl which my body reacts to. He hasn't even touched me and I'm aroused.

We step inside the house, I can't help but feel happy that Jax wants me back. It's too soon though. Finley has only started to get to know him, but then again Finley is the one who keeps begging us to be together. I had to reassure my parents last week that I wasn't pregnant. Seems Finley told them about the sister he keeps hounding me for.

I have just taken my shoes off when Jax backs me up against the wall and claims my mouth again. I need him so fucking bad.

"Be with me again Kendal."

"Isn't it too soon?"

"We belong together."

"I feel the same but-"

Jax grabs onto my face.

"I have waited four years to see you again Kendal. I need you back. "

"But what about Finley?"

"He wants us together as much as I do."

He laughs and it is funny. Looking at Jax, I know I want him back too. I know it's a little soon after him coming back in to my life, but why shouldn't I? I know how I feel. I've felt the same ever since I met him six years ago. Even these past four years were spent apart, nothing changed. I still love him. I don't want to fight it anymore.

"OK."

I whisper.

"Yes?"

"Yes."

"I fucking love you baby."

"I love you too."

He lifts me up and holds me against him.

"You're mine again Kendal."

I moan against his mouth as he kisses me.

"I've always been yours."

This makes him crush me back onto the wall.

"I want you so fucking bad baby."

"Then have me."

He sets me back down on the floor with shaky legs.

"I want you sober the first time."

"I'm not dunk."

I say as I stumble over nothing.

"OK, maybe a little bit."

I hear Jax chuckle and take hold of my hand.

"Come on, let's get you to bed."

Upstairs Jax helps me to undress into my vest and shorts pajama set. Not very sexy but they were already on my bed. I noticed when I wasn't in my bra and thong he took his time to cover me up.

I can now feel the alcohol that I have drank tonight like; it's all hitting me at once. Jax helps me lay down on my bed, I suddenly remember that I have to take my eyelashes and make-up off. Jax doesn't let me move, he goes to grab my face wipes, while I pull my eyelashes off and place them onto my table beside my bed. When I go to reach for a wipe he holds them back. He tells me to close my eyes and I do, then I feel the face wipe across my face. My heart swells. I know he's only wiping my make-up off but I feel so happy right at this minute. It's relaxing and it nearly makes me go to sleep. When he's finished he plants soft kisses on my face and neck, he then turns me so that I'm tucked into his arms. As he smooth's my hair I'm half asleep, I don't know if I'm dreaming or not but I hear Jax whisper.

"So happy I have you back baby. I'm going to take good care of you and Finley."

~Jax~

I don't fall asleep straight away. I'm too happy because I finally have my girl back. Even if she did tell me that she loves me while she's drunk, and after I had a fight with her fucker of an ex; I still can't believe how he spoke to Kendal. I could have fucking killed him.

I hold Kendal against me thinking about what's going to happen now. When would we tell Finley? I fall into a very happy sleep that night, with my girl finally in my arms.

When I wake up I find Kendal looking up at me. We're still in the same position with my arms still around her. Even in my sleep I can never let Kendal go.

"Morning beautiful."

She gives me her breathtaking smile.

"Good morning handsome."

I roll on top of her which makes her laugh.

"Do you remember last night?"

She rolls her big beautiful eyes at me.
"I wasn't that drunk."
"Good."
I kiss her like I'm a starving man and Kendal is my food.
"Mmm. I could get used to this every morning."
"Well this wouldn't be happening if Finley was here."
"I will have to get a lock on your door."
She lightly smacks my shoulder.
"Don't you dare"
"What time's the little monster back?"
"My dad's picking me up at 12:00, I'm having my dinner with my parent's."
I look at the time.
"I have you for three more hours."
"Mmm-hmm."
"Better make the most of it then."

I kiss her again, feeling that new tongue bar of hers. Hearing her little sighs of pleasure spur me on. I tug her top above her head and that makes Kendal grab onto my shirt and pull it off. She groans as her hands glide over my torso.

"Jax."

I know what she wants and I want to give it to her.

"You're mine now Kendal."

"All yours Jax."

She whimpers. I trail kisses down her neck and when I reach her gorgeous tits I can't help but lick her perk nipples I pay special attention to my favourite new piercing of Kendal's on her left nipple.

.

"I need you Jax."

"I don't have any condoms."

She shakes her head and pulls my hardened cock free through the little pocket in my boxers. She licks her lips and my cock twitches in eagerness.

I watch as Kendal slowly lowers her head and flicks my tips with her tongue and fucking hell, that felt good. I groan and she lowers her mouth down my shaft inch by inch. Fuck me! I've changed my mind. Her nipple isn't my favourite piercing of hers, I love it but Kendal's tongue bar is now my fucking all time favourite. The way flicks it and rolls it along the length and my swollen tip makes me tilt my head back. I hold onto her head and pull her down so I'm fucking her mouth.

Before I can explode into her mouth I pull her free. She puts on her serious face.

"Are you clean?"

I don't blame her for asking me.

"I'm clean babe, I always use protection."

The only girl I've ever gone bareback with is Kendal.

"I'm on the pill."

I haven't had sex for so long I'll probably come within minutes.

~Kendal~

I watch as Jax decides on what to do. He's really killing me here. I push him off me and pull down his jeans chucking them on the floor. He doesn't put up a fight, but when I slide down his boxers he starts to protest. I don't listen; I need him inside me now. Even if that means in my mouth, I need him.

With his boxes now down I get a look at my enormously big friend. Oh how I've missed you. It twitches and I look up to Jax's face to see him smiling down at me. I wrap my hand around his thick shaft and hold eye contact with him as I take Jax in my mouth. I watch as his eyes roll back in bliss and hear his groan of satisfaction.

I take him as far as I can go without gagging and work the rest of his cock with my hand because Jax is a very big boy. I've always marveled at how big his cock is. That's probably why I had such a good friendship with it.

I've only had him in my mouth for about a minute when he pulls out of my mouth. Before I can complain Jax rolls on top of me again.

"I think you have too many clothes on."

He pulls off my little shorts and cheekily swipes his tongue along my outer folds. He covers my body with his, settling himself in between my open legs. Jax's hard, defined body makes me feel soft and feminine. He looks me straight in the eye as he slips his hard shaft inside of me. I groan in delight and I see Jax's jaw tense. When he's all the way in he gives me a little peck on my forehead.

"I love you baby."

I feel like I could cry but I manage to hold my tears back.

"I love you too."

I love him so fucking much it hurts. As he pumps his delicious cock in and out it feels like he's reconnecting us. I look at his beautiful face, but Jax stops me from doing that as he kisses me again, I'm glad he does because as he kisses me he picks up the pase. I'm so pleased because I would be screaming louder if he wasn't. Jax grabs my legs and places them over his shoulders, which makes him slide in even deeper.

"Oh God Jax!"

"Feel me baby."

Yes I can feel him alright. He's making my whole body quiver as he plays me like his guitar. Now that Jax isn't kissing me, my passionate sounds fill the room. Jax slams himself into me again and again. I start to feel the burn inside, it's coming but I don't want it to end. It feels so damn good, I thrust against him and meet him pound after pound. With every pump, slam and growl Jax brings my body closer to the edge.

"Come Kendal."

"Oh God."

He reaches down in between our connected bodies and rubs my clit which makes me scream into orgasm. As I'm floating in pleasure I feel Jax fill me with his fluid, which adds to the sensation. His legs are down and on top of my legs; he doesn't attempt to move from being on top of me. We come back down from our high together. I run my hand through Jax's hair and he breaths heavily on top of me. I immediately miss his heat when he lifts up off me.

I open my eyes to see him looking down at me. He's smiling that sexy charming smile that makes me horny all over again.

"I missed you princess."

"I missed you too."

We lay in bed together side by side. We decide to let our friends know that we're back together but not our parents or Finley yet.

.

Chapter 14

~Kendal~

Today is Wednesday, the first time Finley is going to sleep over at Jax's house. I made sure Jax told Max and Leo that he was over because I don't want any random women hanging around while my innocent young son is there. Not that I think they would do that while Finley's staying over.

Before Jax will take him over to his house, he has a surprise for him; an early birthday present. With what we have bought him already he has plenty but I let Jax have his way.

He found a music store out of town that sells child size acoustic guitars. There was no way I was letting him buy an electric one. Jax wants to teach Finley to play and I can't wait to watch.

This is the first time Jax and Finley will be together all day and overnight without me. From what I can tell they're both really excited. Finley has chosen what he wants to pack in his overnight bag and I can't help but feel a little nervous. The way he can be picky with his clothes can be a nightmare in situations like this. He packs a bag to my parents and he still changes his mind in the morning. That's why he has a selection of clothes over there. I just hope for Jax's sake Finley sticks with the clothes he has packed.

Over the last four days Jax and I have taken our new relationship slowly and I'm really enjoying every minute of it. Nothing has really changed, apart from the kisses we steal when we think Finley's not looking and the passionate nights he stays over in my bed until midnight. It's horrible when he has to leave me but until we tell Finley, he has to.

Our friends are really pleased for us. Even Sam, Mark and James seem happy for me and I'm so relieved that they are. I am so proud that they have finally managed to put their differences behind them, they are able to see Jax for who he really is and that he makes me very happy.

I think this happened when they all saw just how amazing Jax is with Finley and they can see how much Finley loves Jax. This has helped them to get over whatever it was they held against Jax and the band.

At 11:00am I know Jax has pulled up because I can hear Finley banging on the living room window and shouting at him. I am so thankful he is finally here to pick him up. Finley woke up at 6:45 this morning and since then; every couple of minutes he has asked me "is it time for Jax to come"

Finlay is so over excited it's giving me a headache!

Normally Jax would have been here earlier but today the band had to attend to some radio interviews. When Jax enters the front door I have a clear view of him, he's standing in front of the sink having just washed the dishes. When he sends me a cheeky wink I can't help but blush. All images of last night rush through my mind.

We have spent every night since Wednesday together and we have enjoyed the bed, floor, wall and my shower very, very much.

Jax and Finley have their cuddle in the hallway and when he comes over to give me a welcome hug he whispers straight into my ear.

"I'm going to miss you so much tonight baby."

Those sweet words make my body tingle with need. I squeeze him hard and whisper that I love him. Jax gives me a kiss that seems way too short for my liking, but that's all I can get with two innocent little eyes here watching us.

When we break apart Finley is looking up at us with a big smile. Why does it feel so weird that our nearly four year old son really wants us to be together? I think we should tell him soon, it's obvious he would be happy about the news. As cheesy as this may sound, I know that this time it is forever. I know I don't want to leave Jax; I only just managed to leave last time because I thought I was doing what was right by him. I can't ever do that again. Not to me, not to Jax and most importantly; I can't do that to Finley.

Maybe as an extra birthday present we should let him know his mummy and daddy are boyfriend and girlfriend. Jax picks Finley up in his arms.

"Right little man, are you ready for an early birthday present?"

Finley's face lights up.

"Yes! What is it?"

"You'll have to wait and see. Go and say bye to mummy."

Finley gets down and runs over to me. While he's hugging me he cheekily whispers.

"Do you know what my present is mummy?"

"Yes."

I whisper back.

"Tell me. I won't tell daddy."

I laugh and hold him back at arm's length.

"It's a surprise Finley. Now go and have a good time with daddy."

I give him a big kiss. I'm always sad when we separate.

"Be a good boy."

"OK mummy."

I smile as I watch him go and collect his overnight bag.

"I wish you could come with us."

I look over at Jax.

"Even if I wasn't at work today I still wouldn't come. You two need your father and son time together without me. You've missed out on enough because of me."

Jax quickly walks over to me and softly wraps his hand

around the back of my neck.

"You need to stop thinking like that. We're all together now."

I look away from his face.

"I can't forget Jax. What I did to you-"

Jax cuts me off.

"I don't want to hear anymore Kendal. I don't think like that, so neither should you."

He gives me a deep kiss before I can speak again.

"Oooooooo! You're kissing!"

We quickly step apart and Finley is right there, wide smile and looking straight at us. Jax and I look at each other then break into laughter.

Be
I wave them off as they drive away in Jax's car, I can't help but think about what I have done to Jax. What I have stopped him from experiencing. How can he be OK with what I did? I know that he thinks about it because I sometimes catch him staring at old pictures of me and Finley. I really want to make it up to him. Maybe Finley's idea of a baby isn't so bad. I know I want to be with Jax for the rest of my life, I know I can't live without him. I won't say anything to him though because that topic of conversation is

way too soon.

~Jax~

I wish Kendal were here to see this right now. Finley is looking at the row of child size guitars with a look of awe. As soon as I told him where we were he was bouncing in the car seat. I just had to buy him a guitar, the way he looked at me with amazement when he watched me play was priceless. A moment I won't ever forget. I knew he would love one of his own and as soon as I found the perfect shop, I had to bring Finley.

The shop was a little out of town but for what I wanted for Finley, it was perfect. Here Finley can get an acoustic guitar that's perfect for his size and it can be personalized however he likes.

Finley points to a black guitar that has red down the sides and under the strings. It's by far the best one here.

"I like that one daddy."

"Are you sure that's the one you want?"

"Yeah. It looks like a rock star one."

He makes me so proud. I let the owner know that it's the one. We're the only three people in here. I didn't tell Kendal that I closed the shop down for me and Finley. She didn't take it well when I did the same for his birthday. The thing is, sometimes it's just easier this way. I didn't want to risk being approached by fans while I'm here shopping with my son for his birthday.

When the owner brings out Finley's choice in guitar it's time to personalize it. He wants his name *'Finley Parker'* scrolled on the red side panel. Not long after I found out about Finley, Kendal and I had changed his surname from Kendal's to mine.

It was Kendal who wanted to change it as quick as possible, of course I wanted Finley to have my last name but I didn't want to anger or hurt Kendal. There was no need to tell Finley about this, because I don't think he would understand what we were telling him.

In white writing on the black front he wants *'Rock Star.'* surrounded by white stars. It's going to look awesome, it would usually take a couple of weeks to complete but I want it finished in time for Finley's birthday on Friday. It's amazing what flashing a little cash can do.

When that's all done, we make our way through the crowd of paparazzi to my car and go to the McDonald's drive through before we head home. While we are at McDonald's Finley turns to look at me all serious looking.

"Are Uncle Max and Uncle Leo at your house?"

"Yes."

"What about their dinner?"

"They'll be fine."

"No daddy, that's not nice."

Admitting defeat I ring Max and ask if they want anything. Of course they say yes and it's not exactly a small order.

"Wow! A lot of food."

"That is because they're pigs."

That makes Finley throw his head back and laugh loudly.

"You are funny daddy."

My heart doubles in size. This little boy. My son, he is bringing me so much joy to my life. Along with his mother these two are giving me more happiness than I ever thought possible. Everybody says that Finley is my double, but at times all I can see is Kendal reflected in Finley. He has her caring nature and her laugh. Just then when he exploded into laughter, he was all Kendal.

When I drive up the private road that leads to the house that I share with Max and Leo, I feel a little nervous. This is the second time Finley has come over; the first time was when Kendal and Finley came to see where I live. It's just beginning to hit me that I have Finley to myself until 4:00pm tomorrow when Kendal finishes work. I know that Max and Leo are also here, but it's different without Kendal. I don't have her to lean on with the parental side of things. This will be good for me. I understand why Kendal wanted to give us some alone time now.

I haven't even parked the car when Max and Leo come running out of the front door. Leo opens the door near Finley and picks him up. I'm very happy that these two get on so great with Finley. I'm glad to finally see a genuine smile on Leo's face for once. I don't know what happened on the night I had a fight with Harley, but ever since then Leo has been in a worse mood than before.

"Hey buddy! What are you doing here?"

Finley chuckles.

"Uncle Leo, I'm sleeping here!"
"Really?"

Finley nods his head quickly.

"You can't sleep in my bed. You snore too loud."

"No I don't! I'm sleeping with daddy."

Leo and Finley make their way into the house. Finley is still in Leo's arms. Max helps me carry the three bags of food inside. Seeing as Finley is here we decide to use the table for once, rather than the sofa. Finley looks over to Max and Leo.

"Daddy said you two are pigs."

He starts giggling to himself. He's such a little snitch. Max looks up to me as I'm biting into my burger.

"So is your dad."

This makes Finley look back to me and laugh again.

"Yep!"

After our food I take Finley up to my room to put his clothes away.

"Am I sleeping in your big bed?"

"Yes, why?"
He makes a funny looking face.

"I don't like sleeping with mummy."

"Why?"

"She likes to have all the cover."

I can't help but laugh. Poor Finley. I can remember just how much she likes the entire quilt to herself.

"Don't worry; I don't take all the covers."

We all spend the rest of the day goofing around.
At 7:00pm Kendal rings me.

"Hey beautiful."

I hear her musical laughter down the phone.

"How has it been?"

"Great. He loved his surprise."

"Aw. I knew he would. Are you sure it will be ready for Friday?"

"Positive."

I tell her about our day together and then let Finley talk to her. All through the phone conversation Finley has a huge smile.

"Hello mummy.......Yes its fun here......Yea! It's a rock star one. I told the man I want my name on it.......Yeah, Uncle Max is rubbish at football."

I listen to all his side of their conversation. Listening to him talk to Kendal makes me want to be with her so bad right now. I've loved spending the last four nights together. It makes me long for us to be a proper family at last. The gift I have for next week can't come quick enough.

Chapter 15

The next morning I wake up to the bed shaking. As I begin to become aware of my surroundings I can tell it's Finley who is jumping and now he had begun chanting.

"Daddy, daddy, daddy!"

At the top of his voice. So this is what Kendal warned me about.

"Finley."

I moan out loud but he ignores me.

"Get up! Get up! Get up!"

"Lie down please Fin."

"It's breakfast time!"

He hasn't stopped bouncing by the way. I rub my eyes and reach for my phone. When my eyes finally are able to focus and I see the time I groan.

"Finley, it's only 7:00!"

"Yes! It's breakfast time!"

Unable to stay in bed a second longer I have no choice but

to get up. I'm glad he manages to sleep so well. I was worried he might be a little homesick and want to go home but as soon as I put him to bed I didn't hear anything from him. You don't know how happy it makes me that he's here with me.

I carry him down to the kitchen. Thanks to Leo, luckily we have the cereal Finley wants. The man can't live without it. After our breakfast and watching cartoons we both go back up stairs to get ready. As I open my door I look back to see Finley standing in the middle of the landing facing the other doors.

"Where's Uncle Max and Uncle Leo bedrooms?"

"Why?"

"They're lazy."

A plan comes to mind so I show him which one is Max's room. When I open the door we silently creep in and see Max lying on top of his covers. Thankfully still in his boxers. I didn't think to check to make sure he didn't have his dick out. I could've scarred my son for life there. Finley shakes his head at the sight of Max and whispers.

"Uncle Max you are lazy."

Then without warning he runs the distance to his bed and starts jumping. I decide to lean back against the wall and enjoy the show. Finley bounces right next to Max who finally begins to stir. He rubs his eyes and that's when Finley starts shouting.

"Uncle Max is lazy! Uncle Max is lazy!"

I can't help but laugh at the horrified look on Max's face as he wakes up to Finley's shouting.

"Finley? Where's your dad?"

Finley just points to me.

"Over there. Now get up you lazy man!"

I didn't think Max would actually get up but like I said the guys love Finley and he has them wrapped around his finger. Much like everyone else. After Max and I watch as Finley does the same to Leo. His reaction was fucking hilarious. As soon as Finley bounced Leo shot up in his bed looking scared shitless.

~Kendal~

After my shift at Bianca's I'm in the staffroom getting my things ready when Tanya walks in for her break. She looks at me and gives me an irritated look.

"Spill."

I'm a little confused.

"What?"

Tanya throws her arms up in frustration.

"You've been staring at me ever since I got here!"

It's true. When Tanya arrived at work I took any chance I could to look over to her to make sure she was okay. I can't help that I'm worried about her.

"Are you OK?"

All I get as an answer from her is a frown.

"Ever since the wedding you just seem down all the time. Don't deny that you're not, you can't lie to us anymore. We can all see it. It's because of Leo isn't it?"

Again she doesn't answer.

"We're just worried about you."

"So you've all been talking about me behind my back?"

"It's not like that. We are worried. Jax said Leo is the same."

Her eyes widen.

"You've spoken to Jax about me too?"

"Only because he told me that Leo is acting miserable as well."

This seems to lessen her anger.

"He is?"

I nod.

"What's going on with you two?"

She shrugs.

"It's nothing."

I feel frustrated. This is the same crap she's been feeding us ever since we noticed the change in her.

"Oh come on! You can't give me that shit. We're friends and I know when you're lying."

"Why should I tell you Kendal? You will just run off to Jax

and tell him everything that I tell you."

That hurt.

"I know what I should tell him and what I shouldn't."

"Right because I forgot you're this happy new couple now."

I can't talk to her when she's acting like this. I know she's hurting so I won't slap her like I want to. Instead I grab my bag and go to walk past her.

"Come and talk to me when you're not acting like a bitch."

When I start to walk past her in a rush she reaches out and grabs onto my arm.

"Wait. Fuck. I'm sorry Kendal."

She does look sorry. Her face has softened and I can see tears line her eyes.

"We just care about you."

"I know that and I love you all but I'm just so fucking confused."

My tough nut of a best friend suddenly looks very vulnerable.

"Just talk to us. We all want you back."

"To tell you the truth Kendal, I don't want to talk about it. I'm sick to death of thinking about that pig headed man. All I will say is that Leo just wants to have another amazing fuck, but because I'm saying no, I've suddenly become interesting. That's all he wants from me and I'm not giving it to him."

She is nearly crying, I just stay silent and watch her. I know what she's saying sounds like Leo, but I know that's not true. Why would Leo be acting as Jax has said just because Tanya's knocked back sex with him? There's definitely something more going on here but I'll have to wait for Tanya to come to me when she's ready. She gives me a friendly hug.

"I'll try not to act like a bitch anymore."

I laugh at that. I'm not so sure.

Half an hour later I'm at home and changed out of my work clothes. All thoughts of Tanya and Leo gone because I'm waiting for my boys. It feels really weird that I'm so nervous to see Jax again. We need to talk about telling Finley about us. I did want to wait until tomorrow but I've been thinking about it non-stop at work and I want to tell him now.

I'm sitting in my living room watching TV when I hear Jax and Finley come in. Finley comes rushing into the room and jumps on me on the sofa.

"I'm back mummy."

We share a big cuddle. I missed him so much. Even though I know he's been with Jax, I just miss him whenever he's not with me. When Finley gives me breathing space Jax gives me an innocent kiss.

It's not long before Finley decides he want to play in his bedroom leaving me and Jax alone. This is probably the only chance I'll get with him alone so I quickly say what I need to.

"Jax. I've been thinking about us and well.....I want to tell Finley."

At first he looks surprised but then he grabs me in a bone crushing hug and then kisses me harder than I thought possible.

"When do you wanna tell him?"

"Tonight?"

"That soon?"

"Well, I thought that you could stay tonight and wake up on Finley's birthday here. With us."

I'm beginning to doubt myself so I quickly add.

"Only if you want-"

I'm sucked into his heart stopping kiss. He needs to stop doing this, I can only hold back for so long.

"Of course I want to."

"I love you."

"God I fucking love it when you say that."

He tackles me on the sofa so I'm now lying down.

"I think I should take you and Finley out for dinner to celebrate."

While me and Finley get ready to go out to dinner, Jax goes home to pack a bag of clothes. I don't want it to look like I'm trying too hard, so I put on one of the blue dresses Jax purchased for me. It's figure hugging but it doesn't show too much. It goes across my chest so there's no cleavage on show, there's no sleeves and it goes just below my knees. I put on my leather jacket and some simple black heels. Dressy casual, perfect. There's no surprise I have no choice in what Finley wears but as usual he looks perfect. He has his black skinny jeans on that are just too adorable. Skinny jeans for a four year old! A thin, dark gray t-shirt with a black and red checked shirt over it. It's open and he has rolled the sleeves up, his black hair spiking everywhere. How does he know how to dress himself like this? It looks like he had a professional choose his outfit. I look at him and smile as he puts on his black Converse, he looks just like a rock star's son.

Jax comes strolling in not long after I'm ready looking delicious. He has his tight jeans on with a black shirt, sleeves rolled up like Finley's. Also in black Converse. He puts his bag down on the stairs and Finley points to it.

"What's that?"

Jax and I both exchange a look and silently agree now is the time. I take hold of Finley's hand to lead him into the living room and sit down beside him, Jax on his other side.

"Finley, we want to tell you something."

He stays silent, Jax picks it up.

"You know how you want mummy and daddy to be boyfriend and girlfriend?"

Finley nods.

"Well....Mummy and daddy are now."

Finley looks between me and Jax. He looks to me when he asks.

"You're boyfriend and girlfriend?"

I smile and nod but really I'm a little scared. I thought he would look pleased but he doesn't look happy or sad. The he catches me off guard and jumps in the air and shouts loudly. He then comes back and wraps and arm around both me and Jax. Finley stops shouting and I feel his body shaking.

At first I think he's laughing but then I hear a little sob. Jax pulls him off us so we can look at him and what I see breaks my heart. He's crying!

"Oh Finley. What's the matter?"

He sobs a little more and I hear the words "so happy" in between them. How adorable, he's crying because he's happy. I was scared for a minute there he had changed his mind. When his tears stop he smiles at us.

"Is that why you and daddy kiss?"

"Yes."

I laugh at him but when he asks his next question I stop.

"Are we living with daddy now?"

"No Finley."

"Not yet anyway." Jax adds.

He looks at me with pure desire and I'd love nothing more than to live with my two boys. As a proper family.

Chapter 16

~Jax~

I wake up the next morning pretty much the same as the day before, only this morning it's fucking better. After Finley went to bed last night me and Kendal didn't waste any time getting to know each other's bodies all over again. That one night was way too long to be apart from her. Before we both went to sleep Kendal advised me to put my boxes back on. I'm glad I did because here we are.

"Mummy! Daddy! Mummy! Daddy!"

Finley chants and does a crazy little dance on the bed. Suddenly the bouncing stops and Finley looks down at me.

"Why is daddy here?"

Kendal and I look to each other.

"I thought you didn't live here daddy?"

Thankfully Kendal saves us.

"We had a sleepover so daddy is here for your birthday."

Finley then does his crazy dance again and shouts.

"It's my birthday!"

Last night was fucking incredible. After we told Finley I couldn't wipe the stupid smile off my face.

When we arrived at the restaurant I wasn't surprised to see some paparazzi waiting. For the first time in about three years I wasn't bothered about them. I was actually happy they were there to capture one of the best nights in my fucking life. I didn't give a fuck that I was smiling like an idiot as I walked towards them, with Finley holding both mine and Kendal's hands. By the way, Kendal was smiling, just like me. She looked so happy and that made me feel like a proud man as we faced the paparazzi.

You could see the confusion on the paparazzi faces because I'm known for not paying attention to them and never stopping to give them an opinion or an answer to their questions. I think the last time I did was right at the beginning when Decoy was first signed. When we got near enough I stopped to pick Finley up and wrap my other arm around my woman.

"Are you and Kendal back together?"

"Is it true you're getting married?"

"Jax why did you hide them?"

The questions went on and on while they flashed their camera's. Instead of answering question after question I just give my statement.

"This is my beautiful girlfriend Kendal, I'm glad to say we are finally back together. At long last. This here is our amazing son Finley. There are no plans for a wedding. Yet. We're here to celebrate Finley's fourth birthday, so if you don't mind."

After we satisfied our hunger for each other I held her all night. The fact today is my boy's birthday makes this extra special. Finley is still bouncing on the bed and singing.

"I'm having a party!"

Kendal smiles up at me. She's looking freshly beautiful,

purple hair all over the pillow.

"I wonder when he's going to stop this."

I pretend to think about it.

"I'm thinking sixteen."

That makes Kendal laugh loudly. The same laugh she shares with Finley.

We both have no choice but to get up. I think we're both excited to start Finley's birthday because we both quickly get dressed. I pull on my loose sport trousers and a plain shirt. Kendal puts on some black leggings and a plain vest top. I have to look away from her arse in those skin tight leggings. Fucking hell, I can see every curve of her backside in those things!

We finally make our way downstairs and watch Finley as he opens his birthday presents. When Finley was sleeping last night I got Max and Leo to bring his presents around. After Kendal told me how he likes to look for them we decided to keep them at mine. Watching him tear them open with a huge smile on his face was emotional.

As Finley's sits in his battery powered Range Rover there's a knock on the door. Kendal runs to answer it and when she returns she's holding a big parcel.

"One more Finley."

He runs over to Kendal and rips it open. When he has it open he shouts.

"Aw yeah! My rock star guitar!"

After a huge breakfast Kendal goes to take a shower so I decide to teach Finley some simple chords on his guitar.

When it's noon, everyone comes to celebrate with Finley. I can't help but feel a little gutted that my parents can't be here. They're on a cruise and can't come home early. I have told them about Kendal and Finley and they're very happy. I was worried they might hold a grudge against Kendal, but they were just happy they finally had a grandchild. I hated having to tell them over the phone but I had to tell them. As soon as they come back I know they will come here before they go home. They have met Kendal a few times from when we first started dating and they loved her. Kendal was the girl my mum bugged me about, but now I have her back again.

Everybody gives Finley his extra presents, he's such a lucky dude. I feel a little bad between all our friends, Finley is the only child. I look around at our friends and think who would have a baby next when my gaze lands on Kendal. She's talking to Sam and Jessica with that happy smile she has been wearing since yesterday. She would kill me if she knew the crazy thoughts running through my head right now.

"So Finley just told me his mummy and daddy are boyfriend and girlfriend."

I turn to the sound of Sophie's voice and see she's standing behind me with Rhys.

"We told him last night."

Sophie gives me a cuddle.

"I'm so happy for you Jax."

Sophie is one of the few people who truly knew what I was going through when I was without Kendal. Rhys pats me on the shoulder.

"Finley also said that mummy and daddy had a

sleepover."

I can't help but laugh and Sophie and Rhys join in.

"Little fucker."

"When are you three moving in together?"

Sophie wiggles her eyebrows.

"I'm working on something."

Which makes her looked shocked so I shake my head at her, letting her know I'm not saying anything more. Rhys saves me from her questioning.

"Look at him, so fucking miserable."

I don't need to look to see who he's talking about but I do anyway. I see Leo standing with Maisy. She is looking at Leo like lost child, but Leo only has eyes for Tanya who is busy talking to Kendal's parents. Sophie shakes her head.

"He's next in line to sort out."

.

~Kendal~

Seeing as all our friends are over at mine, we all make our way to Finley's party at CrazyKids together. All the adults have decided to come along because Jax had told them he's hired the place for the day. Of course they want to have a little play themselves.

Jessica has made Finley an amazing birthday cake as usual, this time in the shape of a guitar.

This year feels so much more different than Finley's previous birthdays. This year my happiness isn't faked. This year, because I'm not worrying about Finley being without his dad, it's a much happier day.

When all of Finley's friends arrive and have been happily playing for an hour, I decide it's time for some food. I go into the decorated party room which has food set out on a long table with small chairs for the children to it on. I go about unwrapping the sandwiches and other party foods when Sam finds me.

"So this is where you're hiding out."

"No, it's dinner time."

Sam helps me by pouring out juice into the little cups while I set a party hat down on every paper plate.

"I'm so happy for you Kendal."

I smile up at him.

"Thanks Sam."

He stands in front of me.

"We all hated seeing you fall apart. I was starting to get worried."

I frown down at the floor. He's right, I was falling apart, but at the time I didn't realize. I woke up every morning and put on a fake smile for my son. The only reason I got up in the morning was because of Finley. He was my lifeline.

After the children have all eaten they run back into the play area and Jax helps me clear up the mess. I'm about to pick up a plate of half eaten food when Jax stops me.

"Leave that."

He grips my waist and spins me around to face him. He captures me in a hungry kiss that makes me forget where we are. Once I've collected my wits and the party room is clear of mess we walk back into the main party area hand in hand. I see some of our friends give us happy looks at the sight of us.

The rest of the party is spent like the first half. I catch sight of Max and Leo racing with Finley on the mini quads. I try my best to catch Finley in the ball pit. You don't realize how hard it is to run in those things!

An hour after the children have eaten, their parents come to collect them and now it's just us adults and Finley. It's our time to play and you can see the excitement on all our faces. Sophie, Tanya and I all go down the bumpy slide together. I get thrown into the ball pit by Rhys. I chase Finley around and Maisy asks me and Jax to go down the three way slide with Finley for a photo. A play fight breaks out in the ball pit which travels outside the ball pit and turns into boys VS girls. Then the balls get forgotten and I don't know who started it, but then it's food that's being thrown instead of the balls. All hell breaks loose and it's a major food fight. Rhys and Jax pin me and Sophie down so Max and Leo can smother food in our faces. Tanya and Jessica manage to cover James and Sam in jelly. Above everybody's laughter I can hear Finley's the loudest.

Jax drove me and Finley here so he comes back home with us. While I run Finley a bath I quickly get changed out of the food covered clothes I'm wearing. When I go back downstairs Jax has changed too and we bath Finley together. Laughing about Finley's day, I look at him and I don't know if it's because it's his birthday or not, but this is the happiest I've seen him.

When Finley goes to sleep that night Jax and I don't waste any time. Seeing as we're both still a little dirty from the food fight we take a shower together. I can't help but trace his tattoos and the hard lines on his stomach. Every time I look at Jax I can't believe he's mine. Jax is the man you dream about. He takes great care of me, he runs his hands over every inch of my body. Finally he washes my hair and after I return the favor.

When we go into my bedroom Jax lightly throws me onto the bed.

"I've wanted you so bad all fucking day."

His words make me shiver and I wonder what he's doing when he lies down beside me. That is until he grabs hold of me and flips me so that my face is above his hardness and Jax's face is between my thighs. He dips his tongue straight in and I close my eyes in delight and when I open them I see his hard cock bouncing in my face. I latch my mouth and rub my tongue bar down his stiff length and I'm instantly rewarded with his deep moan. He dives his tongue deeper into my slickness and we keep at it, beautifully torturing each other in our own rhythm. I can feel myself coming to the end.

"Jax."

He growls and attacks my clit with so much passion I can't concentrate on giving him his blowjob. He dips his tongue in and swipes after, as I come closer to the edge I feel his thumb thrusting inside while his tongue flicks me wonderfully. When my climax comes I have to grip onto Jax's thighs it's so powerful. I'm riding my pleasurable bliss that I'm not aware he has moved us both. We're now both sitting up, Jax on the bottom and me on top, straddling him. My body is so limp that he has to hold me upright. When he slips his delightful cock inside I collapse onto him.

I don't know how I'm going to cope with more. Jax holds onto my hips and controls my body. He slams me down onto him so that he's buried deep within. I let him have his way with me, not that I'm complaining. I don't know how my body can take so much pleasure after that shattering orgasm, but Jax is giving it to me hard and I'm not even screaming. I think my body is taking that much from Jax and taking everything he is giving me. I'm incapable of doing anything else, including making a single sound. My mouth however is hanging open and I can feel my eyes rolling back. He feels so good and I don't think another climax is possible until Jax demands it.

"Come Kendal."

My body responds to his growl, I can feel my climax creeping. How is my body going to take another if it's as powerful as the last? He growls again as he tightens his hold on my hips and slams, slams, slams me down harder.

"Give it to me baby."

I can feel it, I'm coming.

"Now."

And I do. Thank goodness Jax thinks to cover my mouth in time because my body decides it's time to scream and I do so loudly. When my climax takes control of my quivering body I scream into Jax's hand. I feel Jax stop his thrusts as he fills me. I'm not able to move, my body has totally shut down. Jax being the wonderful man he is gently lays me down, whispering how much he loves me. He leaves me for a couple of minutes but I'm too tired to see where he has gone. He returns to clean me, it's a little embarrassing but as he cleans between my thighs he plants gentle kisses on my stomach.

When he's satisfied that I'm clean he joins me in bed but not before pulling back on his boxers. He turns me so my back is along his front then Jax kisses me on the back of my shoulder.

"I love you so much baby."

"Love you."

I manage to say quietly.

"So, so fucking much."

I finally give in and let sleep claim me.

Chapter 17

~Jax~

The past two weeks have flown by. Kendal, Finley and I are becoming closer by the day and I really can't describe how much they mean to me.

Mine and Kendal's relationship is getting stronger too and my father son relationship with Finley feels like it couldn't get any better, but it does.

The band has recorded two songs for our new album and we can't believe how much better it is this time around. This time we're taking our time to create our album, not writing them on a packed tour bus seems to help.

Above everything else, I keep thinking about the night I had sex with Kendal on Finley's birthday. The sex was amazing as usual but after I came inside her I kissed her stomach with a silent promise. There will be another Parker baby, just not yet.

Moving my thoughts away from my wishful thinking I get a little nervous about what I have planned for today. I have a surprise for Kendal. It will benefit all three of us but it's mainly for her. I don't know how she's going to react and I'm shitting myself. I hope she's not going to get angry with me. I didn't spend last night with her because I had to make sure everything was done for today.

As I drive to Kendal's house I think over and over again, I hope she says yes.

~Kendal~

Last night, Jax and I spent the night apart. Just one night apart and I'm craving him so badly. How I managed four years apart from him, I don't know.

He's told me he has a surprise planned for me today. I have no clue to what he has up his sleeve. He did have a cheeky smile on his face when he told me though. I have no idea what we will be doing today so I have a dilemma. How do I dress?

I decide dressy casual that way I'm safe. I look in my wardrobe and laugh then open my other wardrobe. After Jax treated me to all these beautiful clothes they over took my wardrobe, so Jax got me a matching wardrobe for my new clothes. I decide to wear the white Chanel short sleeve shirt and team it with my floaty, leather looking skirt. I tuck my top into the skirt and it stops right at my knees so it's not too dressy looking. If I put my heels on it will look like I'm trying too much so I go for my purple high top Converse.

"Where are we going mummy?"

Finley walks into my room.

"I don't know Finley. Daddy said it's a surprise."

Then we hear the door open downstairs. Finley rushes down to meet him and I follow. When I see Jax at the bottom of the stairs holding Finley in a tight hug the sight makes me feel all warm inside. What did I do to deserve to live happily like this?

When Jax sets Finley down he looks to me and his gray eyes look like they darken in color. My heart rate picks up at his smoldering look. He grabs me in an embrace and holds the back of my head as he captures my mouth. So Finley doesn't hear he whispers.

"You look so fuckable right now baby."

I laugh as he demands another kiss. Finley laughs beside us.

"Daddy loves mummy."

"I love you both buddy."

Jax holds onto my hand and pulls me into the kitchen and sits me in one of the chairs around the table. Finley is right behind us.

"I thought we were going out?"

He sits beside me and looks nervous. Why is he acting so strange?

"I need to talk to you before we go."

I frown at him confused.

"Why?"

Jax clears his throat.

"When we get there, keep an open mind OK? Don't freak out please."

I'm getting really suspicious now. What has he got planned?

"Are we going now?"

Finley asks Jax with his pouty face. Jax stands up and holds his hand out for me. He's acting strange and it's making me nervous.

During the drive I keep quiet. I just look out the window and watch where we are going. We pass Rhys and Sophie's house and now I'm really confused because there's nothing down here but houses where the rich and famous live. Two minutes after we pass Rhys and Sophie's house, Jax stops the car. All I can see outside the window to my side is a high brick wall. A couple of paces in front I can see high metal gates. I turn to face Jax.

"We're here."

I look around outside the window, I can't see anything. Jax chuckles and drives the car so that we are now facing the two huge gates guarding the property inside. I look through the gates from my seat but all I see is a pebbled road leading up to a row of tall fir trees.

"Remember, don't get mad."

I watch as he gets out his car keys from his pocket. Attached to his keys is a little remote control where Jax clicks a button. I hear the clatter of the gates and watch them open. When Jax has the car inside he presses another button and they close behind us.

"Coooool!"

Finley shouts from his seat behind us. Jax continues to drive up the little road and I look out the window. What is he doing? Are we meeting someone?

Surrounding the little road is bright green grass. Jax follows the road right up to the trees and it leads us around through a small gap. When we're on the other side I gasp out loud. This place is absolutely stunning. In front of us is a cream colored huge house. It almost looks like a castle.

We drive onto the pebbled drive which is a square shaped section that runs the whole length in front of the house. Whoever lives here is stinking rich. It's then I notice there are no other cars here. Jax parks the car facing the beautiful house. Big paneled windows scatter the front of the house and right in the middle is an over sized glossy black door.

"What do you think?"

"I think this place is beautiful. Who lives here?"

He gives me a cute little smile.

"We do."

I stare open mouthed at Jax. Did I hear him right?

"That's if you'll both move in with me."

Did he just say what I think I heard him say? Jax has bought this beautiful mansion for us? Our first house together as a family is here? This is crazy!

I don't have a problem moving in with him, we've practically lived together ever since we told Finley about us.

"When did you buy this?"

"The first day I went with you to take Finley to school, I saw this house before I moved in with Max and Leo."

I remember. He drove me to work as well and that was the day he first saw Harley. He's kept this a secret for this long?

Finley whines from behind me, poor guy is probably so bored.

"Can we go in now?"

I look back and nod at him.

"Let's go and have a look at daddy's new house."

I don't miss the flash of pain in Jax's eyes but it's quickly gone. Fucking hell, why did I say that? That made it sound like I didn't want to move in with him. I do, but it's a huge shock.

As soon as Finley gets out he runs around like a mad person. I look around the property. The perfectly cut grass goes all around the house, little bushes darted here and there. I see a garage on the far end of the drive that looks big enough to be a house on it's own. Jax and Finley begin to walk toward the large door so I follow still looking all around me.

When I step inside behind them I stop in my tracks. I'm in total awe. I've only stood in the entryway and if this is the first room I can't wait to see the rest! The entryway is a circular room, very light and open. The bottom of the stairs start to my right and curve up along the wall, they finish in the middle of the room, level with the white banister on the upstairs landing. There are three doors leading out. One to my right, just before where the stairs begin, another in the middle of the room right in front of me and one to my left.

Jax takes my hand in his when he sees me standing still in the open doorway.

"I hope you like it baby."

He then begins to show me around the house and it's not long before I'm in love with this house.

All the way through I can see us three living here and having a great time. It's weird because this house doesn't feel strange and new, it feels like home. I don't know how it can feel like home because my home doesn't have an indoor pool or a cinema room! The living room is huge and there's another living area that looks out to the garden with huge glass doors. I can see that room becoming my reading room. The kitchen is beautiful and very large. It's a kitchen and dining room all in one room. I can immediately see how I want this room to look.

The upstairs is just as impressive, five large bedroom all with their own bathroom. The first bedroom we step inside I know is going to be mine and Jax's room. Not only is it overly big and has his and hers stations in the separate bathroom but it has a walk in wardrobe that's far too big. This house was probably a six bedroom house originally by the size of it. When we enter another room Finley immediately shouts "mine!" as soon as we step in. This room is unreal! It has two floors! It's a normal bedroom and then in the far corner there are steps that lead up to a secret room high in the corner with a slide to come down on. I want this room! We watch Finley use the slide and I wonder over to the big panel window that overlooks the garden. The outside is just as stunning as inside.

We take a stroll out in the garden. It's not as big as Sophie's but it's still a large garden. There is an outhouse to the side of the garden that's overshadowed by trees. It's one floor and looks big enough to be a one bedroom bungalow. Jax reveals this will be his home studio. He shows me you can enter the garage from the inside of the house and when we enter my mouth hangs open.

"This is one huge garage."

To which Jax just shrugs his shoulders. We wonder back into the house and stand in what would be the main living room.

"So, what do you think?"

"The house is amazing Jax but, it's huge. Isn't this going to be too much?"

As amazing as this house is, surely it will cost too much to run and maintain. Jax just laughs at me.

"It's perfect so don't worry about it."

"What about all of the bills?"

He frowns down at me and holds both my hands.

"You're not paying for anything Kendal. I'm taking care of everything."

"Everything?"

"There is one thing I need you to do though."

"What?"

"I want you to decorate it."

"All of the house?"

"However you want. On me of course."

I don't tell him that I already have ideas of how I want to decorate each room. I look around the huge room and think even though this place is extremely large for just the three of us, I can really see us here living happily as a proper family. Jax takes hold of my face.

"Get used to this Kendal. You can have whatever you want. I want you to make this our home. Make this your home."

I can feel the tears building. I can't help it. I know I want this and how can I not love this house?

I can't wait to make this our home. I know it's all quick but why shouldn't we live together? We know we want each other. We've spent too much time apart to waste any more time. There's no reason for me to say no, so I look straight into Jax's eyes when I tell him.

"Yes."

Chapter 18

~Jax~

Did I just hear Kendal right?

"What did you say?"

She smiles at me.

"Yes Jax Parker. I will move in with you."

Finley starts to jump about excitedly.

"Yeah! We're moving into the big house!"

I sweep him up into my arms and then walk back to Kendal and give her a kiss. She has just made me the happiest man alive. Kendal laughs at me.

"Are you happy?"

"You don't know how much baby."

She gives me another kiss and then kisses Finley.

"Do you have any ideas on how you want to decorate? I wanna move in as soon as we can."

I knew that she loved the house as much as I did by the look on her face as I showed her around. Kendal smiles cheekily.

"I've got a few ideas."

I pretend to wince.

"Is it going to cost me a fortune?"

She then laughs and lightly taps my chest.

"You said whatever I wanted remember?"

I hold her against me with one arm, still holding Finley with the other.

"Anything."

We walk around the house again hand in hand. We talk about what each room could be like. There's no need to change the pool room and cinema room. I tell Kendal to not tell me what she has in mind because I want it to be a surprise.

This month has been so hard keeping this a secret from everyone. As soon as I left Kendal at work I went straight to the realtors hoping the house I had loved but didn't buy was still for sale. I have no doubt that Kendal will turn this into a great home.

When we're done Kendal calls Maisy to come over. When they start talking excitedly about all the rooms I see Finley looking really bored so I decide to get me and Finley out of there.

Promising to bring some food back for the girls, Finley and I go for something to eat.

In the middle of eating I get a call from Rhys.

"Hey."

"Hey man. Have you heard from Spencer?"

Spencer is our main band manager. He organizes everything for us.

"No why?"

"He's booked us in the summer festival."

We've never done a festival before. Not that we didn't want to, we just never had time. I'd love to play out to our fans on a hot day outside.

"Great. When is it?"

"Next month. We're on the main stage too."

We finish our phone call and I watch Finley enjoying his dinner. I'm really excited that he will be able to see me play. We have a gig in London soon but they're pretty loud and with all the girls there, I wouldn't want Finley to be around, but a festival he can come to! I'm so fucking excited! He can see me play on stage for the first time.

~Kendal~

I've absolutely loved having Maisy help me transform what I had in mind for the house into a reality.

The day after, Maisy and I had formed my our own little team to help me decorate the house. I wanted it done as soon as possible because as I watched the house become a beautiful home. I was so excited to live here with my boys.

Neither Jax nor Finley had been to the house since we were all there the first time and I'm so nervous to show Jax what's become of the house. I feel so proud at what I have managed to achieve. Jax told Maisy not to show me any prices because I was sure to always go for the cheapest option.

The only opinion Jax had was he didn't want "girly shit" in our bedroom.

I stand in the entry room waiting for them to arrive. I haven't changed much of this room because I loved how open and bright it is. Maisy had suggested adding little hints of gold, which I did and she was right, as always. There is a gold chandelier hanging from the high ceiling in the middle that sparkles brightly and little gold decorations here and there. Not too much but it completes the room.

When Jax and Finley arrive I can't help but smile widely at them.

"Someone's excited."

I roll my eyes at Jax but I really am excited that they're here. I'm more than ready to show them our new home.

I show them the downstairs first. The main living room is in glossy blacks and whites. The carpet is black, which I wasn't sure on at first, but it looks great and I really like it. The little living area, that I can't wait to read in, is decorated like a summer room. It's in light green's and white's but has a cozy feel to it. The sofa just screams at me to jump on it and read. There's a book shelf over on one side that's full of my books and little nick knacks from home. I'm worried Jax won't like it but when he takes a look he gives me a heartwarming smile.

"This is your room huh?"

I bite my lip and shrug my shoulders. Jax lifts my chin with a single finger.

"It's perfect baby."

With his soft kiss I smile back and lead him into the rest of the downstairs rooms. The kitchen is pretty much the same but I changed the cupboards to a thick wood with white shiny glossy fronts. The work tops are the same thick dark wood with the glossy white drawer fronts. One of the work tops can be used as a breakfast bar with white tall stool chairs behind. Since this room is a kitchen and dining area in one huge room I have a wooden table and there's a white floor that can be easily wiped clean. It's bright and open and it's one of my favorite rooms in the house.

"Wow Kendal. You're amazing."

"So you like it so far?"

He stares at me wide eyed.

"Obviously!"

He wraps his arm around my shoulders and we make our way upstairs because Finley is dying to see his room. I can't wait to show it to him and I hope he likes it.

When we step in, Finley gasps loudly. It's all decorated in a rock and roll theme. The walls are a dark gray and red. His bed frame is black and so is his wardrobe and drawers. On his wall is a huge black wall sticker that spells out his name with a guitar laying on top. He even has a clock in the shape of a guitar too. His room is amazing! The best part though is the secret den. It's all painted black on the outside but inside its bright colored and has most of his toys inside of it.

We leave Finley in his room to play while I show Jax our room. Our room is also red but not rock and roll red. Our room is sexy and romantic red with white accessories to brighten it up a little. I did little on the 'girly shit' side but it still has a little feminine touch without being too much. The his and her bathroom is black and white and there was nothing to change with the walk in wardrobe apart from changing the shelving. Jax seems really impressed and I'm so glad he likes it because I love this house so much. At first I was a little sad leaving the home I lived in for four years with Finley, but now I'm so eager to move into our new family home.

Jax doesn't waste any time at all that night we're sleeping in our new beds. We packed a few nights worth of clothing with plans to bring the rest of our belongings the next day.

Finley had trouble going to sleep at first. Not because he was scared or anything but because he was too excited. He loves his new room so much that he wanted to get up and find more or sit in his den. I will probably find him there in the morning.

When Jax and I finally go to bed, he pulls me against him when I lie down beside him.

"You've done such a good job with the house baby."

I smile shyly.

"I'm glad you like it. I was so nervous."

He shakes his head.

"How could I not love it?"

He kisses me softly.

"I love you Kendal."

The look in his eyes takes my breath away.

"I love you too."

The next kiss he gives me isn't so soft. It's hard and full of sexual need. My underwear is soon ripped off with such urgency that I gasp.

"Jax! That was my favorite bra!"

"I'll buy you ten more."

He flicks my nipple with his tongue which makes me forget all about my bra. I reach down between us and grab hold of his pulsing hard cock. Jax then places his hand in between my legs and dips his finger into me.

"You're so wet."

He growls which does delicious things to my body.

"It's all for you."

I sigh and as soon as I say those words he has me on my back. I'm pinned under his mouthwatering body. When he leans down and continues our kiss I grab onto his hair. Jax rams himself into my wetness with so much force that I can't help but scream into his mouth. He continues to slam into me, my eyes rolling back in bliss. My climax soon takes control of my body then Jax flips me onto my hands and knees as I'm still twitching from the intense orgasm.

~Jax~

I claim Kendal from behind while she's still clenching from her orgasm and it feels so fucking good. I almost come right then but her little whimpers of pleasure spur me on. I slip my thumb into her tight rosette and I hear Kendal sharply inhale.

"Oh God Jax."

I feel her body tense and I know she's already close again and I'm not surprised by how fast I'm taking her but I can't help it. I need her. I let my body relax and let the pleasure of Kendal take over me. I know when she comes again because her walls squeeze me tight and milks me as I fill her with my cum.

After we're cleaned up, I hold her tight against me. I gently run my fingers through her hair because I know she loves it. Kendal soon falls asleep in my arms where she belongs. I look down at her, she looks so beautiful. My heart beats so hard it fucking hurts because she means so much to me. Both Kendal and Finley do.

I carefully untangle my arms from around Kendal so I don't wake her up. I pull on my boxers and quietly walk down the large hallway. Two doors down from mine and Kendal's room is Finley's room. I open his door and frown when I see his bed. Finley's not in it and neither is his quilt. I see the light is on in his den through the little window. When I get into his little den I stop and smile. Lying in the middle of the floor, surrounded by his toys is Finley. He's fast asleep, with his quilt over him.

I chuck his quilt down the stairs from his den and carry Finley to his bed. When I tuck him in I stand and look at his perfect little face and give him a soft kiss on the forehead before I go and rejoin my girl in bed.

Chapter 19

One month later

Today is the day Decoy will perform in the festival. Everyone is coming to watch and after there will be a barbecue at Rhys and Sophie's.

This past month has been one of the best months in my life. Living together as a family at last has been amazing. Since moving here, Finley hasn't ran into our bedroom and bounced on the bed in the morning. Instead when we wake up we find him in his den. I made sure to make good use of nearly all the rooms in our new house with Kendal. I look forward to Finley's bedtime so I can finally have my way with her; because lately she loves teasing me all day so as soon as Finley is fast asleep I literally jump her.

We have to be at the festival for 10:00 and as the management have arranged for a limo to take us; everyone is able to ride with us in the limo.

I am sat at the kitchen table with Finley, waiting for Kendal so we can tell Finley where we are going today. We decided to not tell him when I told Kendal what Rhys had told me. If we had told Finley he would have asked about a hundred times a day for the month. He does it with everything that you tell him in advance, and it can be very annoying. So to save us a month of never ending questions we said we would wait until the day.

Kendal gives me a little smile as she places mine and Finley's bacon sandwiches down in front of us.

"Finley?"

He looks up at me as he begins to bite into his food.

"We're going somewhere special today."

Finley has a big mouthful of food so he's unable to talk. Kendal sits down at the table beside us and smiles excitedly at Finley.

"We're going to watch daddy play on a big stage."

Finley quickly swallows his food and stares at me wide eyed.

"With Decoy?"

I laugh.

"Yes Finley."

He jumps up and down in his seat nearly squealing.

"When?"

"Soon."

Kendal answers as she picks up Finley's dropped sandwich on the floor.

All the while Kendal and I get ready to leave; Finley asks again and again when "is time to go?" When the limo buzzes at the house gates I feel like cheering.

I shout for Kendal to let her know and when I see her running down stairs to meet me and Finley at the door, I can't help but stare at her. She looks so fucking sexy that I almost tell her to go and get changed. Almost, I'm not an idiot. She has on a loose fitted black lace jumper, little shorts and her biker boots. Kendal's legs look amazing and as I stare, images of me gliding my tongue along them from last night come to mind. By the time she's beside me I'm panting like a dog.

Luckily Finley breaks my attention away when he sees the limo and he starts to shout and jump about.

On the drive to the festival I listen proudly as he talks excitedly about seeing us play. I can't fucking wait.

~Kendal~

When we sat down in the limo; I sat in between Leo and Sophie. Jax sat straight opposite me, Finley wanted to sit with Rhys and Max at the back.

Throughout the drive to the festival I could feel Jax's eyes on me. Lately I have been finding fun in teasing him all day long, so when we go to bed at night or sometimes as soon as Finley has gone to sleep he can't control himself a minute longer. I know how much he likes my legs so today I wore my little denim shorts to flaunt them. I knew by the way he looked at me when I came downstairs that I had been right to wear them.

While I knew I was holding his gaze I innocently lick my lips. I fight to hold back my smile because then my little innocent act will be over. I cross my legs and include myself in Sophie and Jessica's conversation. I run my hand over one of my legs down to my ankle, just looking like I'm brushing something off my leg. Then because I can still feel his sight on me I adjust my boobs in my bra, making them jiggle a little and bite on my bottom lip.

I can't help but take a little peak at him from the corner of my eye, his jaw looks tense and his eyes are narrowed on me. The look on his face makes me smile and as soon as I do Jax has moved Leo from next to me and sat himself beside me instead.

"You fucking little tease."

He quietly growls into my ear causing all sorts of dangerous reactions to my body.

When we drive into the performing entrance to the festival I'm surprised to see screaming fans holding posters and banners jumping about behind a little fence.

The limo stops beside a huge black bus; I'm guessing it's Decoy's tour bus. I can still see and hear the fans and I can't help but start to feel a little insecure. As each band member stands out the cheering gets louder but when Jax steps out its insane. He turns and holds his hand out for me to help me out the limo. One step away from the limo door Jax pulls me towards him and kisses me. It calms my nerves even though the fans have started screaming and cheering louder. Finley runs from Rhys to hold onto mine and Jax's hands. I can now even hear a few shouts of Finley's name. Being Jax's charming son, Finley just waves a single hand in the air and carries on walking with one hand in mine. Finley isn't affected by this at all.

The tour bus is huge and very modern. When Jax told me

we would be waiting on their tour bus until it was time for the band to make their way to the stage area, I wasn't too thrilled.

I had images of a dirty unkempt, dark bus. I expected a totally stinking mess if I'm totally honest, but I was pleasantly surprised. As I sat down next to Maisy I couldn't help but think about what kind of things that probably have happened on this bus. But as soon as I do start thinking I have to stop myself.

It's not that long when their manager Spencer, a short and round man, informs us that it's time to make our way to the stage area. We all walk together to the sounds of bands and the loud crowds, John and Paul flanking us. Finley holds Jax's hand all the way, jumping along at his side. It's so incredible to watch them both; and I feel so happy for Jax. He hasn't stopped talking about how excited he is for Finley to finally watch him.

We reach the stage area, there are a number of people running around the vicinity and a few security guards scattered about. The loud noise of the band currently on stage fills the entire area. Jax is handed his guitar and begins talking to a roadie. Max, Leo and Rhys do the same and then eventually talk to each other, making themselves into a little circle as they talk privately. I've seen this so many times that it feels like I've returned home.

Finley is now holding onto my hand.

"What are they doing?"

"They're getting ready."

"When are they going on that stage?"

He points to a gap where you can see the stage from the side angle.

"When that band has finished."

It seems only five minutes passes when the band announces that it's their last song. Toward the middle of the song Jax runs over to us and gives me a hard kiss.

"So happy I have you by my side again baby."

He crouches down to Finley's level and holds him in a hug.

"I'm so happy you can watch me Fin."

Finley laughs as he attacks his face with a number of kisses. The band on stage finish and I see a woman walk on stage as the band exits. I hear Jax tell Finley he loves him just as the woman on stage shouts "Decoy!" He gives me a quick kiss on my forehead, tells me that he loves me and runs towards the stage. As the other band leaves and their people follow, we can move closer to watch Jax and the guys perform from the side of the stage.

Jax is absolutely amazing; his energy on stage is just as it always has been. The crowd loves them all; as they cheer loudly, the guys absorb the fans energy and feed of it. In return they are jumping and bouncing about, giving the people all of their sweat and energy. It's amazing to watch, but I can't keep my eyes away from Jax. Finley is beside me jumping around like crazy, singing the words and trying to copy Jax.

Jax's voice sends chills all over my body and I didn't realise how much I missed this but being here I see I missed it so fucking much.

As the show comes to an end my vision is blurred by my tears.

"Daddy is the best rock star mummy!"

Finley shouts and I swear Jax heard him because he turns toward us and smiles. I pick Finley up, kiss his cheek then I silently apologise for keeping him away from this. We watch the last song with Finley in my arms. We both sing the words together along with Jax. When Jax ends Decoys set he turns to face me and Finley and shouts into his mike.

"I love you!"

The crowd screams and I smile back at him as he walks back towards us.

Chapter 20

~Jax~

When our set has finished at the festival, we all head home. We might have stayed a little longer if it wasn't for Finley being there and with Sophie and Rhys wanting to have a barbecue.

During Decoy's performance on stage I couldn't help but to keep looking over at my two favourite people. I was so fucking happy to see Kendal back where she belonged, at my side backstage and cheering me on. I have always loved being on stage, giving the crowd my all but when I looked over and saw Kendal with Finley in her arms as they sang my lyrics, I wanted to run off stage and be with them.

On our walk back to the waiting limo, which was parked near our tour bus, I didn't miss the way men looked over to Kendal as she passed. If Finley wasn't here, I'd be shouting abuse over at them, letting them know what I would do to them if I saw them looking at my girl like that again. My son is here though so I have to make do and give the fuckers a death glare. When they catch me glaring there way, they look away quickly and practically run off. *Yeah that's what I thought, she's Jax Parker's woman.*

The limo takes me, Kendal and Finley back to our house while everyone else goes to Rhys and Sophie's. I take a quick shower, and we get in the Mercedes together. I know

Rhys' is only around the corner but I can't be dealing with paparazzi right now.

Kendal sets Finley in his seat and gets in beside me. Her delicious legs are still on show so when she is sat next to me I reach out and touch her bare thigh. She gives me a knowing smile the cheeky little minx. She has been teasing me all day.

"Did you enjoy the show?"

Finley shouts from behind us.

"Yeah! You were a rock star daddy!"

I laugh and look back at my gorgeous girl. I can't tear my eyes away from her and by the looks of it, Kendal can't take her eyes off me either. Kendal's eyes begin to shine and she nods.

"I loved it."

I grip tighter on her leg.

"I loved you two being there with me."

Little pools line the bottom of her eyes and she whispers.

"I love you."

I take her hand and softly kiss her knuckles.

"I love you too."

Finley starts again.

"Ewwwww."

This makes us both laugh.

"Mummy and daddy are getting married."

Finley sings and Kendal's eyes go wide; I'm pretty sure mine look the same. I look back to Finley.

"What?"

"You said I love you so now you can marry mummy."

He made is sound so simple. What exactly is stopping me?

I look back to Kendal and she's still wide eyed and looks a little pale. She looks scared to death by the idea of becoming my wife.

~Kendal~

With Finley bringing the car into silence, Jax decided it's time to start the car.

As he drives my thoughts spin wildly in my head. It's not that I don't think Jax loves me, I know he does but is he ready for marriage? Maybe that's a step too far for Jax. I would love nothing else to be Jax's wife and share his last name. Jax has a bad boy rocker image so would he want to be seen as a husband and so normal? With Rhys it's a different matter because Rhys is the sweetheart of the band.

As soon as we have parked in Rhys and Sophie's drive I literally jump out of the car. Jax helps Finley and we walk up to the house together. Jax still hasn't said anything.

Rhys is the one to open the door just before we have time to knock. Finley runs straight inside, while Jax and Rhys exchange a few words I follow Finley's example and scamper into the house. I need to rant about my thoughts to someone. With Tanya trying her best to contain her inner bitch over the whole Leo situation; I can't really go to her. So I go about finding Jessica and Sophie. I don't think about ranting away to Maisy because that isn't her at all, so I know not to bother her with my shit.

When I spot Jessica I'm relieved to see she is already talking with Sophie however she's also standing with Maisy and Max. When I quickly approach them they immediately stop laughing as their eyes land on me. Maisy turns an eyebrow up in question and I nod, she knows me so well. Maisy smiles as she huffs and turns to walk away but Max grabs onto her arm.

"Where are you going?"

That's a bit odd of Max but Maisy just shrugs her shoulders.

"Kendal wants to rant. I don't know about you but I don't wanna listen."

She walks away and I watch Max as he doesn't take his eyes off Maisy. He then turns to me.

"Rant?"

"A bitch."

Jessica confirms for him. Max looks a little alarmed.

"You can go."

It's obvious he looks relieved.

"Thanks."

When Max goes Sophie leads us to a secluded part of her garden so we can talk.

"OK, let us have it."

I pour everything out that has been bothering me. From what Finley had asked to the thoughts driving me crazy.

"Obviously he doesn't want to marry me."

Sophie shakes her head at me.

"I think he does honey. Anyone can see he's crazy about you."

"That doesn't mean he wants to marry me."

"Would that really matter?"

Jessica asks me and I think about that for a second.

"No, I suppose not."

"Then what's the problem?"

I turn around and see Jax and Finley playing. It's not a problem at all because I'm perfectly happy already.

"It just hurts."

Sophie grabs a hold on my shoulder.

"Just give him some time."

I manage to give her a small smile. I let my eyes wander around the little party, I spot Tanya and Leo standing face to face. Leo looks like he's begging and could drop down onto his knees at any moment but Tanya's having none of it. Shaking her head at whatever Leo is saying. James approaches and Tanya walks away. I'm now thinking I'm going have to run over and stop a fight between the two but instead I see James pat Leo on the shoulder. If I wasn't so upset at the look on Tanya's face, I would have been so happy at the sight of friendship between my two sets of friends. Maisy slowly strolls up to us with a smirk on her face.

"The bitch fest over?"

"It wasn't a bitch."

Sophie replies.

"No, more like a moan."

Jessica adds.

"I was not moaning."

"You were a little bit."

Sophie laughs and I can't help but laugh along. I stop laughing though when I see Max talking to Tanya. Max has his hand on her shoulder and Tanya is looking down at the floor. The girl looks towards what has caught my attention.

"I think we need to step in before Leo rips Max apart."

I look to Leo and see Maisy is right. Leo is glaring at Max while Jax and Rhys are talking to him. Whatever is happening between those two is definitely not nothing like what Tanya had told me.

Eventually we return to the party and I see Max is watching Maisy as she walks closer to him.

"Seems you have an admirer."

I whisper to her. Sophie who is on the other side of Maisy hears me and looks at Max who still has his eyes on Maisy.

"Interesting."

I can see the match making schemes calculating in her mind. Maisy blushes and peaks up at Max then looks back to me.

"We're just friends."

I'm about to say something but Jax appears and like a silent demand the girls all leave us.

"You OK?"

I feel bad as he looks at me with a little worry in his eyes but if I'm looking a little down then it's his fault for making me feel like this.

"Yes I'm fine. Where's Finley?"

I look around and see him playing with Milly from the wedding.

Jax tries his best to make everything seem OK and I start to relax, maybe I was just moaning and over reacting.

About an hour later Rhys gets everyone's attention. He and Sophie stand in the entrance of their home, the same doors Sophie walked down to him as a bride. Sophie looks a little shy and Rhys stands tall and proud.

"Thank you for coming. There are two reasons why we asked you to come over today."

I look to Jax for an answer but he looks just as confused as me and shrugs.

"Today we played in our home town again and it felt awesome. So to celebrate, we thought we would have a little party. Also..."

He looks down to Sophie who doesn't look nervous anymore. She's beaming as she takes over.

"All of you that are present mean a lot to us, and we wanted you all to hear our announcement at the same time."

Sophie looks up and Rhys and then places her hand over her stomach. Oh wow.

"I'm pregnant."

All of the girls rush up to her and congratulate her.

"Aw Soph, I'm so happy for you."

I feel tears filling my eyes.

"God I've been dying to tell you all but I just wanted you all to know at the same time."

The guys all congratulate Rhys in a typical manly way. I feel so happy for him, when I get my turn I squeeze him as hard as I can.

"You're going to be an amazing dad. I'm so proud of you."

He squeezes me back.

"I hope so."

"I know so."

I don't know if it's me over thinking it and wishing it were true, but I am positive that I keep catching Jax looking at my stomach.

Chapter 21

~Jax~

I felt like shit knowing that I had put that look on Kendal's face, I shouldn't have kept quiet I should have spoken up and told her how much I wanted that. After Finley's innocent question I was shocked into silence, the truth is I want nothing more than for her to be my wife. To be completely mine.

I think I kept quiet because I was also scared. I was scared shitless that Kendal would reject me and run a mile with just the thought of marriage. Why would I not think that? She did run away after she had found out she was pregnant, why wouldn't she do it again if I proposed? So I kept quiet and gave her space to make sure she wouldn't freak out on me. She did look a little on edge.

After she had separated from Jessica and Sophie to go and talk to Tanya that's when I found out how wrong I was. Jessica, my forever inside source told me it was the total opposite. Kendal had kept quiet because she thought I didn't want it. Why would she think I didn't want her to be my wife? Will she ever get over her insecurities and see herself for what she is?

With my new information I try to be the perfect man for the rest of the barbecue to make it up to her. I try and make her see that she is the perfect woman for me. No one else will measure up.

After Rhys and Sophie had told us their great news that

they were expecting a baby, I couldn't help but hope that would be me and Kendal one day. I missed out on all that excitement with Finley, I want that with Kendal. If what Jessica had told me was true and Kendal wanted the commitment of being my wife then why would she not want any more children?

A week has past since the barbecue and I have spent everyday trying to make Kendal feel overly loved. I don't want her to doubt us again. Today I have the perfect excuse to pamper and spoil my princess. Today it is Kendal's birthday. I get up and ready early so I can crack on with my plans.

~Kendal~

As soon as I woke up I noticed two things. Number one is I can smell something sweet and delicious, my stomach grumbles in response. Number two is when I move about on the bed I can feel something under me.

I open my eyes and see that Jax is already out of bed. Weird, he hates getting up in the morning. I thought he might have liked to wish me happy birthday as soon as I opened my eyes.

I sit up in bed and gasp at the sight that surrounds me. No wonder I could feel something under me, covering the mattress all around me are rose petals in all different colours. They are not just on the bed but all over the bedroom floor too, bright colourful petals everywhere.

I look to my side of the bed to see what time it is but I don't look at the time, my eyes have found the reason for the delicious smell I woke up to. On my bed side table is a plate full of freshly baked pancakes. I know they will be perfect,

Jax's pancakes always are. On the tray beside the plate are little bowls full of different toppings and a glass of orange juice.

I don't waste any time and dig straight into them with a big fat grin on my face. I was right, they were gorgeous. I don't manage to eat all of them because there are so many. I get out of bed in my birthday suit and make my way through the pretty petals and quickly get dressed in a white summer dress.

When I walk out my bedroom and through the hallway the house is quiet until I get to the top of the stairs over looking the entry room. I hear a very mischievous giggle. Finley's laughter makes me smile knowing that he will be enjoying this with Jax.

I make my way down the stairs and when I reach the bottom Finley jumps out from the other side of the door. He has a big smile on his face and squeezes my legs.

"Happy birthday mummy."

"Thank you Finley."

I give him a kiss.

"Where's daddy?"

This makes him laugh again. Finley makes the quiet sound by holding his finger in front of his mouth then grabs onto my hand and leads me to the cinema room. I'm thinking he is taking me to Jax but when we arrive the room is empty. Finley takes me to a chair on the back row, there's only three rows of four large comfy chairs. I see a chair with a remote placed on it and a note with the words *play me* in Jax's hand writing. When I look behind, Finley has gone so I sit down and take a deep breath before I press play. I'm shocked at what I see. Jax's sexy smiling face is on the big screen.

"Happy birthday baby. I hope you liked your little surprise this morning."

He laughs a little which makes me laugh along with him. That wasn't a little surprise at all. Which gets me quickly thinking, if that was a little surprise what else has he got planned? Or am I thinking too much into it?

"You will see me soon but first I want you to sit back enjoy your film. I love you."

He winks at the camera and then I stare wide eyed at the screen. I'm shocked at what begins on the screen. It's a video of me and Jax from the first night we met at the house party. I remember that we had flirted most of the night, the party got out of hand and really loud so we went out to the garden. The video is being recorded by Max with Leo by his side, I watch as they spy on me and Jax kissing under the stars. My heart warms, this was before everything had turned complicated. As they creep closer we stop kissing and my laughter fills the silence. Jax looks so handsome. Max walks right up to us and makes himself known.

"Hey Jax, what are you doing?"

"Go away Max."

Max ignores Jax and walks right in front of me, the camera right in my face.

"Hi beautiful, what's your name?"

I giggle shyly. Why would I not? I'm in a garden with three hot guys around me. Obviously I didn't feel more friendship towards Max and Leo then.

"Kendal."

"Pretty name."

Jax pushed Max away from me.

"Fuck of Max."

The video ends with Max's laughter but another starts straight after. It's a video of me and Jax on the beach. The same beach where Leo had taken the picture of us that Jax had printed out for me. This time it's just Jax and me, Jax is recording and it's shaky because he's chasing me. You can hear the wind along with Jax's breathing and my giggles as Jax gets closer. He finally catches me and the camera spins around to film both of our faces. Jax is looking right at the camera but I'm looking at him.

"Got you beautiful."

I kiss his cheek.

"I love you."

Jax looks away from the camera and at my face.

"I love you too."

The video ends and another begins. That's how it goes video after amazing video. I didn't realise I was crying until I had to wipe my face dry. I can't believe he kept all these for all this time. I kept everything to do with Jax and me because I still loved him and never let go. All the time I had thought he moved on but I now know better.

When the videos end our song, Truly, Madly, Deeply by Savage Garden begins to play and a slide show of pictures flash up throughout. Both old and new photos of Jax, Finley and I, some of our friends too. Some pictures are ones that paparazzi had taken and by the end of the song I'm a wet blubbering mess.

The song ends and Jax is on the screen again. God he's so fucking sexy.

"I hope you liked it Kendal. There was never a time when I stopped thinking of you. I've always loved you and I always will. "

His beautiful gray eyes sparkle on the screen.

"Now get of your arse and come and meet me out front. Love you."

The screen goes black. Before I go out there I need to collect myself together, I'm an emotional mess. I can't believe he did all this for me. From the breakfast in bed, the beautiful petals to the magical video he created for me. I can't even begin to think what he has planned next.

All the while I'm walking towards the front of the house I'm smiling. This is my best birthday by far. Not because of what Jax has done but because I'm finally with both of my boys.

I reach the entry room and gather myself before I open the front door. I know they're out there because I can hear Finley laughing.

When I open the front door my eyes widen once again. My mouth drops so far down I think it's going to hit the floor.

Jax and Finley are looking right at me and behind them is a huge white shiny car, the same Mercedes Benz g class as Jax's car but just white and with a big pink bow on the top. Jax has bought me a fucking car for my birthday!

Jax walks up to me because I don't move from the front door, he gives me a cautious soft kiss on the cheek.

"Happy birthday gorgeous, do you like your present?"

"Jax the bedroom and the film were enough.

"I wanted to get you one more present."

I stare at him in disbelief.

"You make the car sound like a box of extra chocolates."

He laughs and takes my hand in his. He leads me closer and closer to the new car on our drive. He looks so excited as he shows it to me. Inside it is all black with little hints of white here and there on the head rest and on the dashboard. It's a stunning car.

"I already have a car though."

Jax and Finley look at each other and then Finley starts to laugh at me.

"Daddy said you would say that."

"Kendal you know how much I hate that thing you drive."

"I love my car!"

"You can still keep the car but I got you one like mine."

There's no reasonable logic to why Jax had gotten me the car. Why would a little family of three need four cars? I can't deny that I am falling in love with the car and it is kind of cute that we will have his and hers cars. I feel sorry for my little Beatle, it's only me that loves that car.

The look on Jax's face as he waits for me to say something makes my decision final. I give Jax a little and I see him relax.

"I love it Jax. Thank you."

"Oh thank God."

He takes me in a tight embrace, he whispers into my ear.

"I thought you were gonna kick me in the balls for a minute."

"I did think about it."

He pulls me back and gives me a heart stopping kiss.

"Do you really like it?"

"I really do. I was just shocked."

"Did you like the flowers mummy."

I kneel down in front of Finley.

"They were lovely."

"I helped daddy."

I kiss him and say thank you. I pick him up and snuggle into Jax's outstretched arm. I can feel tears building.

"The film was amazing."

Jax smiles at me and it's full of love, for me. I see Jax's eyes are glistening a little.

"It was fun making it."

After a quick spin in my new car my parents turn up. They spend a couple of hours with us and when they leave Finley gets his shoes on.

"We're having Finley tonight."

My mum tells me with a knowing smirk.

"You don't need to."

Jax puts his arm around my shoulder.

"I asked them to."

He has that mischievous look on his face so I go along with whatever he wants.

When we're alone I look to Jax for an answer but he just takes my hand and leads me up the stairs. Images of Jax taking me hard in our bedroom gets me all excited and needy but we walk straight past our room. I pout and Jax laughs at me.

Jax stops outside one of the spare bedrooms. He doesn't say anything, just opens the door. I step in but he stays in the doorway.

"You need to be ready in an hour."

I look around the room. There's a dress bag hanging in front of the wardrobe and on the bed are all my hair and make up products. My hair dryer and straighteners and a shoe box. I turn around to face Jax.

"Jax?"

"Just get ready Kendal. It's a surprise."

Then he shuts the door on me. I think about running after him but I hear him shout.

"Only an hour!"

From the other side of the door. So I decide to go along with his plan.

Forty-five minutes later I am showered with my hair now dry and straightened. I haven't seen what's in the dress bag yet, so still in my towel I walk over to it and slowly zip it open. My mouth hangs open in shock and awe. The dress is very sexy and glamorous. It's black with the top part looking like it's covered in glitter. The bottom of the dress finishes short above my knees but the back is longer and almost touches the floor. I need heels and my eyes drop to the box on the bed. I lift the lid and hold in a girly squeal. These shoes are fucking gorgeous! Black with a sparkly strap across the ankle. Jax sure knows how to plan everything.

With five minutes to spare I go looking for Jax and stop dead at our bedroom door. Jax never wears a suit, apart from the wedding. So I'm speechless when I see Jax looking right at me. He's in skinny black jeans, black shirt and black blazer jacket and Converse. Yes they're black too and the sight of him with his clothes, piercings, dark eyes and messy hair he looks dangerous and so very very sexy.

I slowly make my way over to him and the closer I get the darker his eyes become with lust. My whole body shivers in response.

"Fucking hell you look sexy."

"I can say the same for you."

He looks so delicious that I could eat him. I know the exact place I want to eat right now and I lick my lips with hunger. Jax closes what's left of the distance between us.

"Don't do that we need to leave but I fucking want you so bad."

"Take me then."

I need him so bad. I can't wait all night.

"Kendal."

He warns, his jaw is locked and tense.

"Please."

I whisper against his neck and he grabs me against my waist.

"I won't lie when they ask why we're late."

He walks over to the bed with me in his arms. Jax puts me down and turns me so I face the bed and bends me over. He quickly lifts my dress and pulls down my thong. I feel his hands stroke along the curve of my bum and I feel like I'm going to scream. I need him in me now! I pant with need as I listen to him as he frees his cock which I know will be thick and ready for me. Without another second his dives straight in which makes me gasp. My eyes roll in the immense pleasure that is Jax. There's nothing soft and romantic at the minute. Right now we need a good hard fuck and that's exactly what he's giving me. I don't care that I'm making so much noise by the sounds of Jax's groaning he loves my screams. We quickly find our releases and fix ourselves back together with very satisfied smiles.

When we finally get out the door there is a limo waiting for us.

Chapter 22

In the limo I find it very hard not to take advantage of Jax. I need him again and how could I not? He looks so fucking sexy right now.

When I see where we have arrived, I'm shocked. The limo has stopped in front of the restaurant Eclipse. I look to Jax with teary eyes. I don't know why this place means so much to me but it just does. It's only a restaurant, but this is where I first met Jax when he came back. I will always love this place now.

Jax comes closer and holds onto either side of my face.

"What's the matter baby?"

The flash from the paparazzi cameras lights up the inside of the limo and I swallow hard.

"This place."

He smiles at me and it tugs on my heart.

"I know, it's special to me to."

He softly kisses my forehead, cheeks and nose.

"This is where my life started again."

He takes my mouth hard which does nothing but intensify the need I have for him. Jax cruelly pulls away and laughs as I moan. He takes hold of my hand and reaches for the door handle.

"Come on, lets go and give them a photo to be proud of."

He flashes me his charming smile and I swoon. Jax with his damn sexy smiles.

Jax steps out when the driver holds the door open and he turns to hold my hand as I step out. The cameras flash like crazy. Instead of Jax holding onto my waist and leading me past them like he usually does, he stops to face them with his arm protectively around my waist. The paparazzi shout out names to make us look at them instead of others and shout stupid questions. I look up at Jax as he smiles proudly, he looks down at me and without warning he attacks my mouth with raw fierceness. The paparazzi love it and I think we definitely got those pictures to be proud of.

When we go inside we are taken to a private room upstairs again and I'm surprised to see my friends are here. So this is why Jax wanted to be on time. Once everyone has said their hellos and birthday wishes, Max grins over at Jax and I.

"So, why were you so late?"

"We weren't late."

Jax laughs beside me and I freeze. He wouldn't, would he? He threatened that he would.

"She couldn't keep her hands off me."

I can feel my face burning.

"So I had to give her what she wanted."

Jax just shrugs it off like it's nothing. I can't look at the guys. I always talk to the girls about this stuff but not the guys! Fucking hell, I'm so embarrassed.

Luckily for me everyone just laughs it off and we're back to normal. Everyone is dressed up, the girls and the guys looking equally sexy. I don't think they realise how happy this makes me, that they're all here. I'm so relived that Mark, Sam and James put their stubbornness behind them and saw Rhys, Max, Leo and Jax like how the rest of us see them. I'm grateful that Tanya is here and ignoring whatever it is that's between her and Leo so that she can enjoy herself with us tonight. That doesn't mean Leo doesn't stop staring at her with longing. Poor guy.

After a fabulous meal full of laughter we all leave together in the limo. I'm thinking that the driver is taking everyone home, until the limo stops outside a loud thumping club. There's strobe lighting surrounding the building, the whole place just screams money. Just from the outside you can tell this is for rich and exclusive people. There isn't even a line of clubbers waiting to go in. You either know you belong here or not, no que needed. I don't feel very comfortable being here but everyone else seems to be eager to get in and Jax is looking at with an adorable expression, so I keep my mouth shut.

I hear Tanya laugh,

"You think we would just take you to dinner for your birthday? Have a little faith."

When we get out there's the usual crowd of paparazzi and we give them a few seconds of what they want.

"That was awesome."

Maisy squeals in my ear.

When we enter the club my fears of posh snobs fades and I enjoy myself. I see a familiar face from time to time. Jax lavishes me with his loving attention all night. I'm so glad I had burned some of my need for him before we left the house because the way he's been grinding himself on me and kissing me I think I would have dragged him away to a dark corner and had my way with him by now.

When Jax is returning with our drinks I see a very pretty and skinny girl approach him. Jax doesn't look very happy to see her which spikes my interest. Usually with strangers he will be friendly or just shrugs them off. He never looks at them like he's looking at this girl, with hatred. I poke Sophie in her back as she's dancing with Rhys.

"Who's that?"

I see her visibly tense which causes Rhys to see what's wrong.

"Oh shit."

Rhys takes his eyes of the mysterious girl and gets Max and Leo's attention and they frown at the sight of her.

I don't understand what the problem is. It's obvious to me that they know her. The way she touches Jax's arm and sweetly smiles at him boils my blood but Jax just shrugs her of like her touch disgusts him and walks over to me, handing me my drink. He secures his now free arm around me as we face the girl and I don't miss the dirty look I receive from her.

"Kendal this is Naomi. Naomi this is my beautiful girlfriend."

"You're Kendal?"

Her scowl deepens. It's plain to see she wants Jax and that she thinks I'm in the way. Yeah well she's not getting him. Jax is mine so she can turn around and fuck off. Too bad bitch, he wants me.

When she turns her attention to everyone else to say hi, it hits who she is. I thought she looked a little familiar, but now I see it. I definitely know who she is. This is Jax's ex girlfriend. The model! I saw pictures of them everywhere, when they were together and it hurt, badly. I look at her closely now in the darkness of the nightclub.

She's fucking stunningly beautiful, how can I compete with that? She's so much prettier than me. The way she carries herself as she walks away, even though she's stomping in a sulk, she still has grace.

I try and forget all about Naomi, but I can feel her eyes on me as I try and enjoy myself. I can't help but feel insecure, comparing the two of us. I just need to stay strong and show her that Jax belongs at my side, not hers. Besides it's not like Jax looked pleased when he saw her, he looked more angry and disgusted. I need to try and forget all about her and enjoy myself.

~Jax~

I watch Kendal laugh and dance with everyone but I know she's not as happy as she is acting. Everybody is trying her cheer her up because like me, they know something isn't right with her.

I'm not an idiot, I know it's because of Naomi, the fucking bitch upsetting Kendal on her birthday. Why does shit like this always happen in fucking nightclubs?

I look over to Sophie and see she's already looking at me. She looks at Kendal who is standing with Tanya, James and Mark. She's laughing at whatever Mark is saying but it's not real. I see Sophie shake her head at Kendal and then look up to the balcony and frown. I follow her gaze and lock eyes with Naomi, she smiles down at me, but I scowl at her. Why the fuck would I want her over my one and only woman?

When she realizes I'm not going to smile up at her she looks down at Kendal and gives her a nasty look.

I see Kendal messing with her dress, she feels uncomfortable. Why would she let Naomi effect her? She's stunningly beautiful and perfect. Has she not seen how many death glares and threats I've given out tonight at every fucker who dared look at her?

I'm fed up at watching Kendal look defeated. She's supposed to be enjoying today. I make my way behind her and grab her soft body against me. God she gets me so fucking horny without even trying. Kendal gasps and relaxes into me when she realizes it's me.

"You scared me."

I plant a soft kiss on the back of her neck and we start to sway to the fast music. Her friends drift away so we're alone. Kendal leans her head back against my shoulder. She's my world, along with Finley of course and together they make me so happy. I just want to hold onto her and protect her from everything bad. I know without a doubt that if anyone hurt Kendal or Finley or our future children I won't hesitate to kill them.

I need to see Kendal's beautiful face, so I turn her to face me.

"Have you enjoyed your birthday?"

I stroke her cheek and leave my hand there as she smiles.

"I've loved it Jax. You're amazing."

I know we're both drunk but what I need to say would be the same if I wasn't.

"You're so beautiful baby."

I see her bright blue eyes glisten under the flashing lights. I place my other hand on her other cheek and kiss her.

"I mean it. I only need you. I can't live without you."

We stay like that for a while. We dance and I hold her against me, I whisper sweetness into her ear and nobody disturbs us. I need her badly, I have to get her home now.

~Kendal~

I laugh as Jax drags me over to my friends to say goodbye and out to the limo. Jax doesn't allow me to sit on the seats instead he pulls me onto his lap so I'm straddling him. As we are driven home we kiss with pure hunger. We need each other so badly I'm afraid that we can't wait to get home. I can't control my body as I grind against Jax's hardness under his jeans. The driver needs to hurry up, I need Jax right now I can't even think straight!

As soon as the limo pulls up in our drive we jump out and Jax quickly asks the driver if he can go back and wait for the others. I would have felt sorry for the driver if Jax hadn't pushed me through the front door and slammed me up against the wall of our entry room. He takes my mouth one more time and then drops down onto his knees in front of me. He kisses each leg as he takes off my shoes. Jax rolls up the front of my dress and looks right at me as he slides his tongue along my thong. He's deliciously teasing me and Jax growls as he rips my thong away. Before I can shout at him for destroying another item of my underwear his tongue silences me as he flicks my clit. I forget all about the stupid thongs and I can think about nothing else but the pleasure Jax is giving me with his tongue. He places one of my legs onto his shoulder so he can access me better and oh my god I'm so glad we're alone because my panting is so loud. It's not long until his talented tongue brings me to my climax and with my body still weak with pleasure Jax picks me up with my legs wrapped around him.

Jax carries me to our bedroom which is still covered with rose petals. A romantic setting to all the dirty things he is going to do to me.

Jax throws me down onto the bed and petals flutter everywhere but he doesn't even notice. I have his full attention and he strips me from my dress. He leans over me and kisses me, the hardness of his shirt sending blissful sensations through my hard nipples.

Without taking his eyes away from me he strips at the end of the bed. The sight of his ripped muscled body and the intense look he is giving me has me squirming with need as I crave for his cock in me. He leans over me and starts to kiss me. I whimper with need, I have to have him soon. His kisses travel from my lips down to my jaw and all down my neck where he pays special attention to the swell of my breasts. With a lick of my nipple Jax lifts both my legs onto his broad shoulders and slowly sinks himself into my core. When his balls deep he quickly pulls out and then slams back into me.

"Jax."

I plead and he gives me exactly what I need. He pounds in and out of me with such fierceness I feel like I can't breathe. His cock feels amazing, so good that I climax again and then he flips me onto my stomach and slams into me again.

"Can't. Get. Enough."

He growls while he slams into me again and again. I moan into the bed sheets. I've orgasmed twice now, surely I can't again. He stretches me wonderfully and I enjoy the feeling of us together again. I won't ever run again. I couldn't survive it. I didn't think it possible but his rhythm picks up and I know he's reaching his climax too. He reaches under me and tugs on my nipple which stirs my pleasure again and I can't believe that I want to cum again. Three times? I haven't managed three times before but I know Jax won't stop until I reach my third. He lets go of my nipple and reaches for my clit instead and that does the trick. My body convulses and I fall into a whirlwind of pleasure that I can't handle. I try and fight it but with another flick of my wetness it completely takes over my body. It feels fucking amazing and I shout Jax's name into the bed sheets as he fills me with his hot liquid.

We stay in that position for a couple of minutes, unable to move. I don't think I can make my body move. That last orgasm made my body shut down with shock. I feel Jax pull out and he cleans us both. I know he likes to take care of me like this so I don't complain when he does it anymore. He helps me to get under the quilt, well I say help, he did all the work. I felt too weak. Jax chuckles as he settles down beside me.

"It's good you're a little thing."

"It's your fault."

Which makes him laugh again. He wraps his arm around me and turns me to face him. I cuddle into his warm chest and breathe him in. Jax kisses the top of my head.

"I love you."

"I love you too."

Chapter 23

Three months later

Being back with Jax these past few months have been some of the greatest moments I have had in a long time. Finley couldn't love his dad anymore and he's the happiest I've seen him too. It seems I was wrong when I thought he was happy enough with just me. Seeing him now while we're living the family life in our new house makes me see how much he was missing out on before.

Since we have moved into our new beautiful home, Finley hasn't woken me once by jumping on the bed, which is lucky for Jax. He loves his new bedroom and secret hide out too much for that to happen now.

I no longer feel insecure either. I know how much Jax loves me so I am enjoying my life now how I should have always been. My birthday was absolutely amazing and I can't believe I let a girl like Naomi ruin it for me. That night Jax proved to me just how much he craves my body as much as I do his.

Speaking of exes, I'm pleased to say that I haven't seen Harley since the day of his fight with Jax. About a month ago his tattoo place turned into a clothing boutique and I didn't even feel sad at all that he left. After the horrible words he said to me, I will never forgive him.

Tanya and Leo still haven't solved anything but I think that's all on Tanya. She won't listen to anything Leo has to say.

Finley is spending his Saturday night at my parents and I'm

driving in the dark because Jax has asked me to meet him. I'm a little bit nervous as to why he's asked me to meet him. The closer I get to him, the more scared I get because lately Jax has been acting a little strange. It seems like he's been preoccupied and a little jumpy. I can't wait to put an end to it all and finally hear what he has to tell me. I hope it's not too bad because I have something to tell Jax as well.

~Jax~

Kendal is going to be here any minute and I want everything to be perfect for when she arrives.

I've been planning this day for as long as I have loved Kendal, but I've never known how to do this or where the perfect place would be.

This week when we took Finley to the park, it suddenly hit me. The perfect place would be mine and Kendal's secret little garden. We still escape there from time to time so we can be alone. Even though Finley is back at school, we still get visits from friends and family and that takes away from our private time together. As soon as I knew where I wanted to do this, I got in touch with Maisy and all week I've been planning everything.

Now, as I stand in our secret garden that Sophie and Maisy helped me with, I know it's the perfect place I wished it would be.

Some people might think it's a little too soon but I'll just tell them to go and fuck themselves. I can't wait any longer and I know what I want.

~Kendal~

I pull up in the parks car park and look around my car and smile to myself. Even though I was a little mad at Jax for buying me this car I drive it everywhere. It's sad to say that I don't even drive my Beatle anymore but I just can't bear to sell it.

I set out my car and jump when I see Max and Leo approach me.

"Jesus! You two fucking scared me!"

They laugh and I shake my head. Jax had told me to come alone so why are they here? They both tuck each of my arms in theirs and they walk on either side of me. It seems like they can't stop smiling as we walk across the park to the direction of mine and Jax's secret garden.

"What's going on?"

Leo shrugs his shoulders.

"I don't know what you mean."

I look to Max.

"Why are you here?"

"We couldn't let you walk through the park in the dark alone, could we?"

That's true. I would have been a little freaked out but that doesn't answer my question.

We reach the little opening in the bushes to the little garden hidden away. I can see through the opening that it's lit up a little.

"What's happening?"

I turn around to face Max and Leo but they have already started walking back, so I slowly make my way into the little garden and gasp at the sight.

The surrounding trees and little bushes have sparkling fairy lights dangling from them. There are more along the benches and they light the small area in a soft glow. It's bright enough that I can see white roses have been pushed into the bushes and trees by their stems. Also covering the grass are white rose petals. It looks so romantic and I think I could cry. I can't believe Jax has planned this for me.

Jax smiles at me and he melts my heart. What have I done to deserve a man like Jax who makes me feel so adored?

Jax closes the distance between us and takes my hand. He guides me into the middle of the garden and gives me another little smile. I watch as Jax's eyes look all over my face while he softly strokes my hair.

"What's going on Jax?"

He sweetly kisses me.

"I love you Kendal."

"I love you too."

I interrupt him and he chuckles.

"I know baby. When you left me, I just existed. I didn't feel alive. No matter how many fans had shown up to our gigs when we went out on tour. Without you all of it didn't mean anything."

I hope he's going to flip this speech around because it's making me feel like shit what I had put him through. He softly touches my cheek and plants a kiss on my mouth.

"But then I found you and my life started all over again. All I could think about was getting you back. Then, you told me I was a dad and I couldn't believe my luck."

If I remember correctly, I didn't exactly tell Jax he was Finley's dad. It was more like I shouted it at him while I was a blubbering mess.

"You gave me the family I've wished to have with you since the day you left me. That day I met you, you took my breath away and you still do that now every day."

Suddenly Jax isn't standing in front of me anymore. He has dropped down onto one knee at my feet. My eyes widen at what I think he's about to do. I can't stop the tears that start falling down my cheeks.

"Kendal, I've loved you for six years. I will keep on loving you every day of my life. Please say yes and be my wife."

Jax actually looks nervous as he looks up at me. I can't believe what is happening. I was so scared telling him my news but Jax asking me to marry him has made this perfect.

~Jax~

Kendal still hasn't answered me and she has started to cry. Shit!

Have I upset her bringing up our past like that? Have I gotten this all wrong?

I thought this place was the right place to propose to her. She is still crying so I grab her into my arms. This isn't how I imagined this going. I thought she would scream yes and jump into my arms.

"I'm sorry."

I whisper against her hair. Kendal looks up at me and she looks so adorable with her wide blue wet eyes. She sniffles.

"Why would you be sorry?"

"You're crying. I thought I upset you."

I'm fully confused now. If I didn't upset her then why is she crying?

Kendal steps away from me and starts to look a little worried. She smiles but it's small and she still has tears strolling down her cheeks.

"Jax I have something to tell you. I've been trying to tell you all week but you looked a little preoccupied and now I see why."

She glances around the garden and her face brightens up.

"It's gorgeous Jax."

I appreciate that she likes it but all that I can think of is that she hasn't said yes.

"So here it goes."

She releases a long deep breath.

"I'm pregnant."

All of the air rushes out of me and I can't take my eyes away from Kendal. I feel like I should jump up and down and shout at the top of my lungs. I feel that happy but instead I hold it in.

"Jax?"

Kendal looks a little scared now. My eyes travel down to her stomach. Did she really tell me that she is pregnant?

"Say that again."

She bites on her lip.

"I'm pregnant."

I smile widely. I'm so fucking happy right now.

"That's what I thought."

I reach over to her and hold her precious little body against me. Then I quickly loosen my hold on her because I might hurt the baby. Shit, she has my baby inside of her growing. Kendal's pregnant with our second child but this time I will be with her every step of the way. I hold on to her legs and swoop her up in my arms, ignoring her gasp.

"Jax what are you doing?"

"You need to sit down and relax now that you're carrying my baby."

She rolls me eyes.

"Is this how it's going to be?"

"I'm going to make sure you and the baby are safe."

"Jax, I'm fine."

I don't care what she says. I carry her to the lighted bench and carefully place her down on it.

"So are you OK with this?"

I place my hand on her belly in amazement.

"I'm so fucking happy Kendal."

I look up at her and those tears are still there. I kiss her without moving my hand away from her soft belly.

"So we're going to do this?"

She quietly asks.

"Of course we're doing this."

She happily smiles at me.

"I love you."

"I love you too."

I kiss her a little more because I can't help myself.

"You make me so happy."

I remove my hand and squeeze her tight.

"Shit! The baby! Are you OK?"

She laughs and then looks straight into my eyes.

"Yes."

I have a feeling she's answering more than one question.

"Yes?"

I can only hope. Kendal leans in close and whispers against my mouth.

"Yes Jax Parker. I will marry you."

Without another word, I attack her mouth. Kendal has made me the happiest fucking man alive. I still can't believe I have an amazing son like Finley, and she's pregnant with another child of ours and finally she has agreed to be my wife! I'm a lucky fucking man.

This time around I'm going to take good care of Kendal and our unborn baby. I will take over with most of Finley's care so Kendal doesn't have to do it all. Kendal will have the best of everything now and the world better get ready for another Parker baby. If I have my way, it won't be the last either.

Thank you for reading Rockstar's Girl, I hope you liked reading Kendal and Jax's story.

The third book in the Decoy Series, Rockstar's Angel, will be Tanya and Leo's story. There is no release date yet.

Please leave a review on Amazon, Goodreads or Smashwords.

https://www.twitter.com/KTFisher_Author

https://www.facebook.com/#!/pages/KTFisher/490003474414733?fref=ts

Made in the USA
Charleston, SC
05 November 2013